"I only need to look at you to want you, *mia bella...*"

Sentenced to stillness by that startling admission, Isla gazed up at him, barely crediting that she was in his arms in a bed.

"Stop thinking so hard," Alissandru urged her, a fingertip smoothing the frown line forming between her delicate brows.

The heat of his big, powerful body filtering through her pyjamas made her feel warm and secure. He actually wanted her. Alissandru Rossetti *wanted* her and somehow that made Isla feel less alone.

"Are you warm enough now?" Alissandru enquired silkily, a hand sliding beneath her top to splay across her midriff.

Her breath snarled up in her throat at the feel of his big hand against her skin. She couldn't think straight and an instant of panic claimed her because she had never been in such an intimate situation with a man. Her brain whirred at a frantic pace because she knew that Alissandru would expect sex. And why not, another little voice chimed in the back of her head. Why not? *Why shouldn't she?* She was finally with a male who made her heart beat so fast she felt breathless. And shouldn't that be celebrated rather than denied or suppressed?

Lynne Graham was born in Northern Ireland and has been a keen romance reader since her teens. She is very happily married to an understanding husband who has learned to cook since she started to write! Her five children keep her on her toes. She has a very large dog who knocks everything over, a very small terrier who barks a lot and two cats. When time allows, Lynne is a keen gardener.

Books by Lynne Graham

Harlequin Presents

Wedlocked!

Claimed for the Leonelli Legacy
His Queen by Desert Decree

Christmas with a Tycoon

The Italian's Christmas Child
The Greek's Christmas Bride

Brides for the Taking

The Desert King's Blackmailed Bride
The Italian's One-Night Baby
Sold for the Greek's Heir

Vows for Billionaires

The Secret Valtinos Baby
Castiglione's Pregnant Princess
Da Rocha's Convenient Heir

Visit the Author Profile page
at Harlequin.com for more titles.

Lynne Graham

THE ITALIAN'S INHERITED MISTRESS

Recycling programs
for this product may
not exist in your area.

ISBN-13: 978-1-335-41988-0

The Italian's Inherited Mistress

First North American publication 2018

Copyright © 2018 by Lynne Graham

Printed in U.S.A.

THE ITALIAN'S INHERITED MISTRESS

CHAPTER ONE

'THAT'S IMPOSSIBLE... I don't believe it!' Alissandru Rossetti erupted from his chair in the midst of the reading of his brother's will, rigid with outraged disbelief. 'Why tjhe hell would Paulu leave that little slut anything?' he demanded of the room at large.

Fortunately, his mother, Constantia, and the family lawyer, Marco Morelli, were the only parties present because all attempts to contact the *main* beneficiary of the will had proved fruitless. Disconcerted by that revealing word, 'main', Alissandru had merely frowned, thinking it would be just like his late brother Paulu to have left his worldly goods to some do-good favourite charity. After all, he and his wife Tania had died together and their marriage had been childless and Alissandru, his twin, had no need of any inheritance, being not only the elder twin and owner of the family estate in Sicily but also a billionaire in his own right.

'Take a deep breath, Alissandru,' Constantia urged, well acquainted with her surviving son's sizzling temper. 'Paulu had the right to leave his estate where he wished and we do not know that Tania's sister is deserving of so unpleasant a label.'

Alissandru was pacing the small legal office, a form of behaviour that was distinctly intimidating in a confined space because he was several inches over six feet tall, a lean, powerful figure, dressed in one of the elegant tailored black suits he favoured. That funereal colour had earned him the nickname 'The Raven' in the City of London, where his aggressive and hugely successful business instincts were famous, as befitted a renowned entrepreneur in the new technology field. Pacing that office, he reminded the family lawyer of a prowling tiger penned up in a cage.

Not deserving? Alissandru thought in outrage, recalling that little red-headed teenager, Isla Stewart, at his brother's wedding six long years before. At barely sixteen years old, she had been rocking a sexually provocative outfit, parading her nubile curves and shapely legs in a clear sexual offer to the highest bidder, he reflected in disgust. Later that day too, he had seen her emerging from one of the bedrooms in a dishevelled state, only moments before one of his cousins left the same room, straightening his cuffs and tidying his hair. Obviously Isla was just like her sister, Tania, who had been brazen, wanton and dishonest.

'I was not aware that Paulu was in any form of contact with Tania's sister,' Alissandru admitted curtly. 'No doubt she pulled the wool over his trusting eyes as easily as her sister did and wheedled her way into his soft heart.'

Very real grief fractured Alissandru's hard driven drawl as he spoke because he had loved his twin a great deal and could still, even six weeks after the helicopter crash that had claimed the lives of both Paulu and Tania, not quite believe that he would never ever speak to him again. Even worse, Alissandru could not shake the guilt of knowing that he had been powerless to *protect* his brother from that designing harpy, Tania Stewart. Sadly, Paulu's last years had been deeply unhappy, but he had refused to divorce the sleazy underwear model he had married in such haste, believing that she was pregnant... only, surprise, surprise, Alissandru recalled cynically, *that* had proved to be a false alarm.

Tania had gone on to destroy his brother's life with her wild extravagance, her shrewish tantrums and, finally, her infidelity. Yet throughout those excesses, Paulu had steadily continued to adore Tania as though she were a goddess amongst women. But

then, unhappily for him, Paulu had been a gentle
soul, very caring, loyal and committed. *As unlike
Alissandru in every way as day was to night.* Yet
Alissandru had treasured those stark differences
and had trusted Paulu in a way he had trusted no
other living person. And although he was enraged
at his conviction that yet another Stewart woman
had somehow contrived to mislead and manipulate
his brother into drawing up such a will, there was
yet another part of him which, sadly, felt *betrayed*
by his sibling.

After all, Paulu had known how much the family estate meant to Alissandru and yet he had left
his home on the Sicilian estate and all his money
to Tania's sister. A lottery win for the sister, a slap
in the face for Alissandru even though he knew his
brother would have sooner cut off his hand than hurt
him. Paulu, being Paulu, however, could never have
dreamt that so tragic an accident might take both
his and his wife's lives together, clearing the way
for Paulu's sister-in-law to inherit what should never
ever have become hers.

'Paulu visited Isla a few times in London during
that period that…er…' Contantia hesitated, choosing
her words with particular tact '…that he and Tania
were separated. He was fond of the girl.'

'He never mentioned it to me!' Alissandru bit

out explosively, his dark eyes flashing and his lean, darkly handsome features clenching hard at the image of yet *another* Stewart woman having woven her seductive, cloying charm over his impressionable brother in pursuit of profit. Paulu had always been a soft touch for a sob story, Alissandru conceded grimly.

Speaking for himself, however, Alissandru had never been that foolish. He liked women but women *loved* him, hunting him like a rare breed because he was rich and single. In his younger days he had heard every sob story going and once or twice, in his inexperience, had even fallen for such ploys, but it had been years since he had been that naive or imprudent. These days he chose his lovers from his own stratum in society. Women with their own wealth or very demanding careers were a safer bet for the kind of casual light affair in which Alissandru specialised. They understood that he wasn't ready to settle down and practised the same discretion that he did.

'Knowing how you felt about Tania, Paulu wouldn't have mentioned it,' his mother pointed out gently. 'What will you do?'

'Buy Paulu's house back from her...what else?' Alissandru pronounced with an angry shrug at the infuriating prospect of having to enrich a Stewart woman yet again. How many times had he paid

Tania's debts to protect his brother and shield him from her insatiable demands? But what else could he do in the present? Tania was dead and buried and her sister had not even bothered to attend the funeral, all attempts to contact her directly at her last-known address having failed. That fact alone really said it all about the weak bond between the sisters, didn't it?

'We'll have to track Tania's little sister down,' Alissandru breathed in a raw driven undertone of menace.

Isla blew on her frozen fingers, the gathering wind chilling her face below her woolly bobble hat as she fed the hens in haste and gathered the eggs. She would have to bake to use them up, she thought cheerfully, and then she immediately felt guilty for having a happy thought when her only sister and her brother-in-law were dead.

And even worse, she wouldn't even have *known* that it had happened, had not a kind neighbour driven over a week earlier to break that tragic news in person. Her aunt and uncle, who owned the Highland croft in Scotland where Isla was staying, but who were currently visiting her aunt's family in New Zealand, had read on the Internet about the news of Paulu and Tania's death in a helicopter crash. They had immediately contacted their neighbour and had then phoned to ask if Isla wanted them to come home so that she could travel out to Italy.

But what would have been the point in that trip when she had already missed the funerals? Isla asked herself heavily. It was the great sadness of her life that she had never got to know her only sibling. Of course, they had grown up apart and Tania had been ten years older, and Isla was the daughter who was an unplanned and not very welcome late arrival following their father's premature death. Their mother, Morag, already struggling to survive, had headed down to London with Tania to find work while accepting her own mother's offer to take care of her new baby until such time as the little family of mother and daughters could be reunited.

Only unfortunately that reunion had never happened. Isla had grown up in the same Highland croft as her mother had with grandparents who were effectively her parents. Morag had made occasional visits at Christmas, gifting Isla with vague memories of a soft-faced woman with red curly hair like her own and a much taller, leggy, blonde sister, who even as an adolescent had blossomed into a classic beauty. Tania had left home at a very young age to become a model, and not long afterwards Isla's mother had passed away from the kidney complaint she had long suffered from. Indeed, the first time

Isla had communicated directly with her sister had been when Tania phoned the croft to invite Isla to her wedding in Sicily.

Isla had been embarrassed that her grandparents were not also being invited but the elderly couple had insisted that she go alone because Tania was generously offering to pay for her kid sister's travel costs. Being fair-minded people, her grandparents had also pointed out that Tania had never had the opportunity to get to know *any* of them and that they were all next door to being strangers even if they were bound by blood.

Isla still cringed at the memory of how out of her depth she had felt attending that opulent wedding with all its important moneyed guests and of the unpleasant experience she had suffered when cornered by a predatory older man. But, worst of all, the longed-for connection with her only sibling had signally failed to materialise from her visit. Indeed, Tania's attitude to life in general had shocked Isla.

'No, you can thank Paulu for your invite,' Tania had breezed. 'He said I had to have *some* family member present and I decided a teenager was a far better bet than the boring old fossils in the croft Ma used to rattle on about. I'm moving *up* in life with this marriage. I don't want poverty-stricken relatives with a thick Scottish brogue reducing my status in our guests' eyes!'

Tania had merely been outspoken, Isla had decided forgivingly, the product of a liberal and far less old-fashioned upbringing.

'That girl ran wild,' her grandma had once insisted. 'Your mother couldn't control her or give her enough of what she wanted.'

'But what *did* Tania want?' Isla had asked in her disappointment after her sister's wedding when there had been no mention of the sisters ever meeting again.

'Och, the only dream that one ever had was to be rich and famous.' Her grandma had chuckled. 'And by the sound of the wedding you described, that pretty face of hers got her exactly what she always wanted.'

Only that hadn't been true either, Isla reasoned wryly, recalling her next meeting with her sister several years later, after she too had moved down to London. Her grandparents had died within weeks of each other and her uncle had taken over the croft. Her uncle had urged her to stay with them but, after months of having helped her grandmother nurse her grandfather while he was dying and still sad over the loss of them both, Isla had believed that she needed to move out of her comfort zone at the croft and seek independence.

'Paulu misrepresented himself,' Tania had insisted with scorn after announcing that she had left her husband and the marital home. 'He can't give me what he promised. He can't *afford* to!'

And shortly after that, Paulu had come to visit Isla in her humble bedsit to seek advice about her volatile sister. A lovely, lovely man, she thought sadly, so much in love with Tania and so desperate to do whatever it might take to win her back. Her eyes stung as she thought that at least Paulu *had* got the love of his life back before their deaths, *had* reclaimed that happiness before fate had cut their respective lives brutally short. She had liked Paulu, had actually got to know him much better than she had ever got to know her sister.

Had Paulu followed Isla's feisty advice on how to recapture Tania's interest? She supposed she would never know now.

In the snug croft kitchen, she fed the turf fire and shed her outdoor layers with relief. She loved being at the croft, but she missed her city social life with friends. Living where she had grown up meant that even a cinema trip to Oban required extensive planning and a very long drive. In another few weeks, though, she would be heading south again, her promise to her relatives fulfilled. Her aunt and uncle were lovely people; however, they were childless and had nobody but Isla to rely on if they wanted to leave home. It was over twenty years since her aunt had last visited New Zealand and Isla had been happy to help to make that dream come true, especially when that request had come at a time when the café where she had long worked as a waitress was closing and the rent had gone sky-high on her bedsit.

Her uncle's sheep and hens couldn't be left to take care of themselves, especially not in winter or when bad weather was expected, she reflected, casting a nervous glance out at the grey laden sky: heavy snow had been forecast.

She still smiled while watching her dog, Puggle, daringly nestle his tiny body in beside her uncle's elderly and increasingly deaf dog, Shep, the collie who herded the sheep. Puggle adored heat but the little dog was Isla's most impractical acquisition ever. Abandoned on a road somewhere near the croft, he had turned up shivering and starving the week Isla had arrived and she didn't know how on earth she was going to keep him when she returned to London, but his perky little wagging tail, enormous eyes and ridiculously huge ears had sneaked into her heart before she'd known what was happening. He was a very mixed breed with perhaps a dash of chihuahua and poodle because, besides the ears, he had a very curly coat but he also had very short legs and odd spotty black-and-white colouring. Regrettably, it seemed nobody was searching for him because she had notified the relevant authorities and had heard nothing back from any source.

The noisy sound of a helicopter overhead made her frown because the sheep hated loud noises, but she already knew, having checked, that the herd was safely nestled in the big shelter in their pasture, their reading of the temperature as good as any forecaster's. Minutes later, when she was brewing a cup of tea, she was startled when Puggle began barking seconds before two loud knocks thundered on the sturdy wooden front door.

Assuming it was her uncle's nearest neighbour, who had kindly been keeping an eye on her in the isolated croft, Isla sped to the door and yanked it straight open, only to fall back in shock.

It was him... Alissandru—Paulu's brother—the insanely *hot* and gorgeous twin who had knocked Isla for six the first time she'd seen him when she was a naive teenager. There Alissandru was, inconceivably, on the croft's doorstep, jet-black hair ruffling in the wind, dark eyes set below level ebony brows, flawless classic features bronzed by a warmer climate. A strikingly beautiful male, Isla had thought at that wedding while he stalked about the place like a brooding volcano, emanating the most extraordinary intensity of emotion. But Tania had *hated* Alissandru, she reminded herself ruefully, blaming Alissandru for everything that went wrong in her marriage to his brother.

Alissandru focussed on his quarry, Isla, dressed unexpectedly in a long tatty sweater and gym pants, not even shoes on her tiny feet. A woman down on her luck, he decided instantly. Why else would she be back in the family home in the back end of nowhere? An explosion of red curls tumbled down to her slight shoulders, eyes the same purplish blue as violets huge against the porcelain perfection of her skin, her full plump pink lips slightly agape. Another beauty like her evil sister, Alissandru reasoned, refusing to react in any way to the sudden surge of desire. He was a man with all a man's physical weaknesses and responding to a lovely face and beautiful hair was simply proof of a healthy libido, nothing to beat himself up about.

'Er… *Alissandru*?' she questioned incredulously, doubting her recognition because his arrival was so very surprising. They might have been linked by their siblings' marriage but she had never actually spoken to Alissandru before because he had regally ignored her at that long-ago wedding.

'May I come in?' Alissandru demanded imperiously, stifling the urge to shiver even in the black cashmere overcoat he wore over his suit.

Isla remembered her manners and stepped back, muttering, 'Of course…of course. It's freezing, isn't it?'

Alissandru scanned the humble interior, unimpressed at the sight of the one large cluttered room that acted as kitchen, dining and living area. Yes, definitely down on her luck when she was living in such a dump. Some man had probably got wise to her and thrown her out, he thought without hesitation. He was quite sure that the news of her inheritance would make her day and it galled him to be the one forced to make that revelation.

'Er… I was just making tea. Would you like a cup?' she asked hesitantly.

Alissandru flung his handsome dark head back, leaving her uneasily aware of how tall he was below the low ceiling above. His seemingly dark eyes flared to a vivid gold that was stunning below the lights she had on to combat the winter darkness that folded in so early in the day this far north. Unable to stifle the need, she stared, transfixed by those amazing eyes, gloriously fringed and accentuated with spiky inky lashes. Hurriedly, she turned her attention to making a pot of tea, every brain cell scrambled by his appearance into sheer stupidity as she grasped what she should have been saying first.

'I'm so sorry about your loss,' Isla muttered uncomfortably. 'Paulu was a very special person and I
liked him a great deal.'

'Did you indeed?' Alissandru flared back at her,
eyes sparking bright as the sun in his darkly handsome features, an oddity in his stance and intona-
tion that struck a wrong note. 'Tell me, when did you
start sleeping with him?'

In total shock at that offensive question, Isla froze.
'I beg your pardon?' she mumbled as she made the
tea with her back turned to him, thinking she must
have misheard him.

'I asked you when you began sleeping with my
brother. I'm genuinely curious because guilt would
explain a lot,' Alissandru admitted grittily, wishing
she would turn back round again because he wanted
to see her face.

'Guilt?' Still very much at sea as to what could
possibly have brought Alissandru Rossetti to her
door to abuse her with such horrifying enquiries,
Isla gave up on the tea-making and flipped round.
'What on earth are you talking about? That was a
disgusting question to ask me about the man who
was married to my only sister!' she snapped back at
him, colour flushing her triangular face, the colour
of both anger and embarrassment.

Alissandru shrugged a broad shoulder as he took

off his heavy coat and draped it over the back of a chair at the kitchen table. 'It was an honest question. Naturally, I'm curious and I can't ask Paulu.'

A slight quiver in his accented drawl attracted Isla's attention to the reality that Alissandru had been hit very hard by the loss of his twin, much harder than she had been hit by the loss of a sister she had only met on a handful of occasions. Alissandru Rossetti was grieving, and her anger dwindled a little in response to that awareness.

'I don't know why you would even think to ask me a question like that,' Isla admitted more levelly while watching him as though he were an unexploded firework still fizzing dangerously.

Paulu had once told her despairingly that Alissandru could not comprehend the love that Paulu had for Tania because he had never been in love and lacked the emotional depth to even fall in love, but Isla, at only her second look at Alissandru, thoroughly disagreed with that belief. In Alissandru, Isla saw a highly volatile male who literally *seethed* with emotion, every flashing tautening of his features, every spark of brightness in his extraordinary eyes telegraphing that reality.

He stood poised there below the stark light above him, blue-black hair gleaming with the gloss of expensive silk, the smooth hard planes of his flawless face the colour of bronze and doing nothing to hide the strength of his grim jaw line or the angle of his arrogant aristocratic nose, while the faint shadowing of stubble growth darkening the skin round his mouth only highlighted the sensuality of his chiselled lips. Heat mushroomed inside Isla, increasing her discomfiture.

So, she genuinely *didn't* know about the will? Did he look that stupid?

Alissandru tensed, hating the role forced on him by circumstance, wide shoulders straightening, long, powerful legs bracing with instinctive distaste. 'I asked that question because in his will Paulu left everything he possessed in this world to *you.*'

Isla's lips fell open in disbelief and she stared back at him in silence for several seconds before stumbling into speech again. 'No…no, he couldn't have done that…for goodness' sake, *why* would he have done that? That would be crazy!'

Alissandru hitched an unimpressed ebony brow. 'And you're still trying to say you didn't have sex with him? Not even when he was getting friendly with you while he and Tania were separated? I'm sure only a purist would condemn you for loosening the knicker elastic at that point when he was legally *almost* a free man…'

Isla finally unfroze with those deeply offensive

and aggressive words still echoing in her incredulous ears. She marched over to the door and dragged it wide, ushering in a blast of icy air that made Alissandru Rossetti shiver. 'Get out!' she told him fiercely. 'Get out and never come near me again!'

Impervious to the command, Alissandru merely laughed. 'Yes, let's take the gloves off, *cara*. Let me see the *real* Isla Stewart!'

Puggle was growling soft and low and circling Alissandru's feet while being ignored.

'Out!' Isla said again with biting emphasis, blue eyes purple with fury.

Still as a granite pillar, Alissandru surveyed her with cynical amusement, much as though he were watching an entertaining play. Maddened by that lack of reaction, Isla grabbed up his fancy overcoat and pitched it out of the door onto the frozen ground outside. *'Leave!'* she repeated doggedly.

Alissandru shrugged again with blatant unconcern. 'I have nowhere to go until the helicopter comes back to pick me up in an hour's time,' he told her.

'Then you should work at being a politer visitor. I've had enough of you for one day!' Isla replied with spirit. 'You're the most hateful man and I'm finally seeing why my sister loathed you.'

'Do we have to bring that whore into the conversation?' Alissandru asked so smoothly she almost missed the word.

And Isla just lost it at that point. Her sister was dead and she deeply regretted that fact because it meant that she could no longer hope to attain the relationship she had longed to have with Tania. His lack of respect for the departed was too much to be borne and she rushed at him, attempting to slap him, getting caught up instead by two powerful arms that held her back.

'You bastard…you absolute bastard!' she shouted at him in tears. 'How dare you call Tania that when she's gone?'

'I said it to her face as well. The married man she deserted Paulu for was neither the first lover she took nor the last during their marriage,' Alissandru informed her smoothly, and then he released her again, pressing her firmly back from him as though even being that close to her was distasteful. 'Tania slept more often with other men than she did with her husband. You can't expect me to sanctify her memory now that she's gone.'

Isla lost every scrap of colour at those words and backed away in haste from her visitor. *Was it true?* How could she know? Tania had always done what she *wanted* to do, regardless of morality or loyalty. Isla had recognised that disturbing trait in her sibling and had refused to dwell on it, telling herself that it was none of her business because she had been keener to see similarity rather than a vast gulf of understanding stretching between herself and her sister.

'Paulu would've told me,' Isla muttered in desperation.

'Paulu didn't know everything that she got up to but *I did*. I saw no reason to humiliate him with the truth,' Alissandru confessed harshly. 'He suffered enough at her hands without me piling on the agony.'

And the wild defensive rage drained from Isla in that moment. What on earth were they doing? Fighting over a troubled marriage when both parties had since passed away? It was insanity. Alissandru was grieving, she reminded herself reluctantly, bitter as hell about his twin's need for Tania when clearly he himself—in his brother's shoes—would have dumped Tania the first chance he got. He was not a forgiving man, not a man capable of overlooking moral frailties in others.

'Oh, go and fetch your coat back in, for goodness' sake!' Isla urged him impatiently. 'We'll have tea but if you want to stay under this roof you will not insult my late sister again…*is that clear?* You have your view of her but I have my own and I will not have you sullying the few memories I have of her.'

Alissandru studied her set face. It was heart-

shaped, full of determination and unconcealed exasperation. In all his life no woman had ever looked
at Alissandru Rossetti as Isla did at that moment. As
if she was thoroughly fed up with him and being the
bigger person in her self-control and practicality. Her
bright eyes challenged his, her head at a defiant angle
as she awaited his response. Alissandru retrieved his
coat. *Per Dio*, even inside the house he was cold!

An odd little creature, he reasoned as he scooped
up his coat with a frown. No glamour, no groom-
ing, no flirtation or fawning either. He didn't *drink*
tea! He was Sicilian. He drank the best coffee and
the purest grappa. It was, however, possible that in
a temper he had been ruder than was wise in the circumstances, he conceded grudgingly. He had a very
bad temper. He knew that; everyone knew that about
him and made allowances. She didn't, though—she
had talked down to him as though he were an angry,
uncontrollable child. He was enraged by that little
speech she had made; Alissandru's lean dark features
froze into icy proud immobility and he stepped back
indoors to head straight for the smoking fire. On his
passage there, however, something bit at his ankle
and he bent down with a Sicilian curse to smack
away the little animal with the sharp teeth set into
his leg.

'*No!*' Isla thundered at him, charging across the

room to scoop up the weird little dog but only after slipping a finger into its mouth to detach its resolute teeth from Alissandru's silk sock and the bruised flesh beneath. 'Puggle's only a puppy. He doesn't know any better.'

'He *bit* me!' Alissandru snarled.

'You *deserved* to be bitten and bitten *hard*!' Isla told him roundly, cradling the strange little animal to her chest as if it were a baby. 'Stay away from him.'

'I don't like dogs,' Alissandru informed her drily.

Isla dealt him an irritated glance. 'Tell me something that surprises me,' she suggested just as drily.

Huge ears set wide above his curly head, Puggle rested big round dark eyes on his victim from the safety of Isla's arms and if a dog could be said to smile, Puggle the puppy was smiling.

CHAPTER TWO

CLAD IN HIS COAT, Alissandru lowered himself reluctantly into a chair by the kitchen table. The silence was uncomfortable, but he refused to break it.
It didn't help that he had never been so cold in his
life or that Isla was still running around in bare feet
and clearly much hardier in such temperatures than
he was. His body wanted to shiver but, macho to his
very fingertips, he rigorously suppressed the urge.

Watching Isla's quick steps round the small
kitchen area that encompassed a good half of the
claustrophobic low-ceilinged room, he absently and
then more deliberately found himself taking note
of the surprisingly full curves that rounded out the
unflattering clothing she wore. Her sister Tania had
been tall and model-thin but, being both small in
height and curvy at hip and breast, Isla had a very
different shape. The sort of shape Alissandru much
preferred in women, he acknowledged grudgingly,

momentarily becoming rigid as his body found something other than the intense cold to respond to while he struggled to curb that male weakness.

Even so, his response didn't surprise him because Isla was beautiful, even if she was rather less flashy and far more of a natural beauty than he was accustomed to meeting. She wasn't ever going to stop the traffic, he reasoned with determination, but somehow she constantly drew a man's attention back to the delicate bones of her face, the vivacity in her eyes and the sultry fullness of lips that would inspire any man with erotic images. *Any* man, Alissandru told himself insistently, noting the fine scattering of freckles across her fine cheekbones, even more naturally wondering if she had any anywhere else.

His mobile phone rang, uncannily loud in the silence.

'My goodness, you get reception here!' Isla exclaimed in surprise. 'You're lucky. I have to drive a mile down the road to use my mobile.'

The call was a welcome interruption, however, throwing Alissandru out of a rare moment of introspection and thoughts that thoroughly irritated him. He leapt upright and pulled out his phone with the oddest sense of relief at that sense of being connected with *his* world again. But, unfortunately, the call brought bad news and sent Alissandru straight to the window to stare out broodingly at the big fluffy snowflakes already falling and drifting as the wind caught hold of them.

'The helicopter can't pick me up until tomorrow,' he breathed grittily, annoyance and impatience gripping him. 'Blizzard conditions will hit this evening.'

'So, you're stuck here,' Isla concluded, wondering where on earth she was supposed to put him because there was only one bedroom and one bed and no sofa or anything else to offer as a handy substitute. Usually when she stayed her uncle and aunt borrowed an ancient sofa bed from their neighbour and set it up downstairs for her use but in their absence she had been sleeping in their bed.

'Is there a hotel or anything of that nature around here?' Alissandru enquired thinly.

'I'm afraid not,' Isla told him ruefully, setting his tea down by his abandoned chair. 'We'd have to drive for miles and we could easily get trapped in the car somewhere. We don't go out unless we have to in weather like this.'

Alissandru expelled his breath in a hiss and raked agitated long brown fingers through his luxuriant black hair. 'It's my own fault,' he ground out grimly as he swung back to her, his lean, strong face grim. 'The pilot warned me before we took off about the weather and the risk and I didn't listen.'

With admirable tact, Isla compressed her lips on the temptation to remark that she wasn't surprised. Alissandru Rossetti had a very powerful personality and she imagined he rarely listened to the advice of others when it ran contrary to his wishes. Evidently, he had wanted to see her today and no other day and waiting for better flying conditions hadn't been an option he was prepared to contemplate. Now his impatience had rebounded on him.

'You can stay here,' Isla announced wryly. 'And I'm sure we're *both* absolutely thrilled by the prospect.'

An unexpected glimmer of amusement flared in his eyes, lighting them up with pure gold enticement. Isla wondered why nature had bothered to bless him with such beautiful eyes when most of the time they were hard and cold with sharpness and suspicion. She shook away that bizarre thought and instead tried to concentrate on what she could defrost from the freezer to feed him.

Alissandru sat back down and manfully lifted the mug of tea, his mother's training in good manners finally kicking in. But even as he did so he was wondering if he should simply have asked for coffee because he had never before been in a situation, aside of his brother's marital problems, where he was forced to make the best of things that were bad. He supposed he was very spoilt when it came to the luxury of choice because the Rossetti family had always been rich. It was true that Alissandru's business acumen had made his nearest and dearest considerably wealthier, but he still had to look back several generations to find an ancestor who had not been able to afford the indulgent extras of life. The tea proved not to be as horrible as he had expected and at least it warmed him up a little.

'Where will I sleep?' Alissandru enquired politely.

Isla rose in haste. 'Come on, I'll show you,' she said uncomfortably, leading the way up the small twisting staircase.

Alissandru's gaze flickered over the three doors opening off a landing the size of a postage stamp. 'That's the bathroom,' she told him, opening up one of the doors. 'And this is where you'll have to sleep,' she added tautly, opening up a room that was rather larger than he had expected and furnished with a double bed, old-fashioned furniture and a fireplace.

'Where do you sleep?' he asked.

'This is the only bedroom,' Isla admitted, side-stepping the question. 'There used to be two but my uncle knocked them into one after he found out that they couldn't have children. He felt the empty bedroom next door was a constant reminder they didn't need.'

The arctic chill in the air cooled Alissandru's face. 'There's no heating up here,' he remarked abstractedly, wondering how on earth anyone could live with such a privation in the depth of winter.

'No,' she conceded. 'But I can light the fire for you,' she offered, biting her lip when she saw him struggle to kill a shiver and recalling the heat of the Sicilian climate, as foreign to her as extreme cold appeared to be to him.

'I would be very grateful if you did,' Alissandru said with unusual humility.

Isla thought ruefully of all the to-ing and fro-ing up the stairs carting logs and coal and stiffened her flagging resolve. He was a guest and she had been brought up to believe that, if it was possible, guests should be pampered.

'I'll go for a shower...if there's hot water?' Alissandru studied her enquiringly, recognising that there was nothing he could take for granted in such a poor household.

'Lots of hot water,' Isla assured him more cheerfully. 'But you have no luggage so let me see if there's something of my uncle's that you could borrow,' she added, heading for the chest of drawers by the window.

'That won't be necessary,' Alissandru asserted, his nostrils flaring with distaste at the thought of wearing another man's clothing.

'My uncle wouldn't mind and he's tall like you,' Isla argued, misinterpreting his response and assuming that he had sufficient manners not to want to be a nuisance. She rifled through several drawers and produced a pair of worn jeans and a husky sweater that looked as though it had seen better days before the last world war, settling both items on the bed. 'You'll be more comfortable in these than in that suit. I'll go downstairs and sort out something for dinner.'

'Thank you...' Alissandru forced out the words. 'Considering what I said when I arrived, you've been surprisingly kind.'

A delicate coppery brow raised as she spun back to look at him. 'I don't think you consider what you say very often,' she admitted with a sudden spontaneous smile of amusement that lit up her heart-shaped face like a glorious sunrise. 'And you're completely out of your depth in this environment, which makes me more forgiving. I was just as ill at ease in your home in Sicily.'

'*Dio mio*... I thought we made you welcome.'

A tide of colour rose up beneath her fair skin, making Alissandru study her in fascination and move several steps closer to stare down at her.

'Oh, my goodness, of course you did. I stayed in a wonderful bedroom and the food and everything was incredible,' Isla babbled, belatedly conscious that she might have sounded rude and unappreciative of his hospitality and alarmingly aware of his proximity because he was so very tall and powerfully built. 'But it wasn't my world and I was a fish out of water there. I'd never even been abroad before, never seen a house like yours except on television…you know, everything in your home was unfamiliar…and rather unnerving, to be honest.'

Alissandru scanned the tiny pulse flickering wildly just above her delicate collarbone and he wanted to put his mouth there. He was convinced that her heart was hammering out the same fast nervous beat because naturally she recognised the heightened sexual awareness that laced the atmosphere between them. *Of course*, she did, he told himself cynically. She was twenty-two, no longer a teenager, precocious or otherwise, and an adult woman in every sense of the word. With that thought driving him, he lifted a hand to tilt up her chin, gazing down into startled dark blue eyes and the surge of pink suddenly brightening her cheeks. She blushed. When had he last met a woman who blushed? It was simply that fair skin of hers, doubtless telegraphing the existence of the same erotic thoughts that were currently controlling him.

Would she, wouldn't she? Alissandru asked himself but he rather thought the answer to the suggestion of sex would be yes. He always got the answer yes from women, couldn't remember when he had last been rejected, and the chemistry between him and Isla Stewart was indisputable. He didn't like it, indeed he despised it, but the same powerful drive that had hardened him to steel with arousal was what kept the human race alive and it was appallingly hard to resist for a man unaccustomed to having to deny such a normal urge. He pictured her spread across the bed with its ugly patchwork duvet set...pale and lush and pink and *freckled*? Sex would be one useful way of keeping warm and it would provide entertainment into the bargain, Alissandru rationalised with ease.

Alissandru slowly lowered his handsome dark head, giving her time to retreat. But Isla was frozen into immobility, disturbingly preoccupied by the tightening of her nipples and the low pulse of heat thrumming at the centre of her body. Once or twice before she had experienced such glimmerings of awareness with other men but the attraction had always vanished the moment they actually touched her, convincing her that the fertile scope of a woman's imagination had to explain a lot of encounters that were later regretted. Yet now, when her every cautious instinct with his sex urged her to back away from Alissandru, sheer curiosity kept her where she stood because she wanted, inexplicably *needed*, to know if it would be the same with him.

And he kissed her cheek and her temples and brushed his mouth with astonishing gentleness across hers in an exploratory sortie. 'Tell me now if you want me to stop.'

Isla quivered inside her skin, entrapped by feelings she had never felt before, her body alight from those fleeting caresses, the sudden heat in her pelvis making her squirm. And the *scent* of him that close… Oh, dear heaven, how did she describe that faint evocative scent of cologne and musky masculinity that made her positively quiver with powerful awareness?

'Do it,' she heard herself urge wantonly, and the breathless sound of her own voice shook her.

With a smothered laugh, Alissandru crushed her parted lips beneath his own and sensual shock engulfed her because with one passionate kiss he inflamed her, and her hands lifted to curve round his neck to steady legs that had turned bendy as straws. He scooped her up against him with a strength that initially disconcerted and then, ultimately, thrilled her. His tongue darted into her mouth, flicked, dallied, twinned with hers and extraordinary sensation exploded throughout her body, switching it onto an altogether higher plane of response. A choked little sound escaped low in her throat, and he set her down and stepped back from her, so aroused by that hoarse little noise she had made in the back of her throat that he had to call a halt.

'I need that shower. I've been travelling all day, *gioia mia*,' Alissandru intoned thickly, hot golden eyes locked to her flushed and embarrassed face. 'Now I look forward to the evening ahead with anticipation.'

And with that unanswerable assumption that Isla knew full well that she had encouraged, he vanished into the bathroom. Her bare feet slapped down the stairs in a hasty retreat and she caught a glimpse of herself in the mirror at the foot, hair a messy bonfire of curls, her face hot enough to fry eggs on.

Why *had* she encouraged him? A foolish thing to do when he had to stay the night and was the kind of man accustomed to easy, casual sex. At the wedding, Tania had gossiped about Alissandru's many affairs and even though Isla knew she shouldn't have listened, she had because at the age of sixteen she had been mesmerised by his looks and commanding charismatic presence. But she was twenty-two now, she reminded herself ruefully, and supposed to be beyond such silliness. Even so, she couldn't lie to herself. When the opportunity had presented itself, she had grabbed at it and him, desperate to know what it would feel like when a man of his smooth sophistication and high-voltage sensuality kissed her. And now she knew and she also knew it would've been better had she not found out.

He knew how to kiss—he really, *really* knew how to kiss—but of course they weren't going to take it any further. She was related to Tania and he had hated her sister, it seemed, as much as her sister had hated him. No, nothing more would happen, she told herself, striving to feel relief at that conviction instead of shamelessly disappointed. As Tania had once said, her kid sister needed to get out there and find a life, but Tania had been so much more confident and experienced, freely admitting that she much preferred the company of men to women.

Isla, however, had been raised with Victorian values that tripped her up when she tried to fit into the real world. Most of the men she had met or dated had expected sex the first night, and those that hadn't demanded sex as though it was a right hadn't appealed enough to her for her to experiment. And then there had been her off-putting *first* experience of male sexual urges, she conceded, recalling in disgust the older man who had followed her up to Tania's bedroom and cornered her at that Sicilian wedding. Ill equipped to deal with such an incident back then, she had been frightened and revolted when he'd tried to touch her where he shouldn't have and that episode had, for years, made her very wary of being alone with men.

She had stayed a virgin more from lack of temptation than for any other reason, however, hoping and trusting that eventually the right guy would come along. But her brain knew very well that Alissandru Rossetti would *never* be that guy. He had hated her sister and was clearly predisposed to be prejudiced against Isla as well. Alissandru would be the last man alive likely to offer Tania's kid sister a relationship.

Apart from anything else, Alissandru didn't *have* relationships with women. He wasn't looking for one special woman or commitment. He wasn't interested in settling down. Catching herself up on that revealing thought train with a mortified wince, Isla crept reluctantly out into the teeth of a gale and driving snow with the coal bucket while scoffing at her own foolishness. Alissandru kissed her once and *she* started fretting about their lack of a future as a couple. How ridiculous! He would run like the wind if he knew! Her grandma had raised a young woman out of step with the modern world, imprinting her with a belief pattern that others had long since abandoned.

And Alissandru would be the worst possible man for her to experiment with, she told herself impatiently. No, she would light a fire in the bedroom for him, cook him a hot meal and keep her distance by dozing in an armchair overnight. If she had roused his expectations of something more than a kiss, and she was convinced that she had, she would make it clear that nothing was going to happen. And with the options a man as gorgeous as Alissandru had in his life, that disappointment was hardly going to break his heart. In fact, it was much more likely that Alissandru had only come on to her in the first place because she was the *only* woman available. Her nose wrinkled. His apparent attraction to her suddenly no longer seemed flattering.

Isla trundled kindling, coal and logs upstairs and lit the bedroom fire while listening to the water running in the bathroom. There would be no hot water left for her use: he must've emptied the tank. The back burner in the fire was efficient at heating the water but Isla was trained to spend no more than ten minutes under the shower.

Warm for the first time since arriving in the frozen north of Scotland, Alissandru dried himself vigorously with a towel and stepped out onto the icy landing in his boxers, passing on through into the bedroom at speed where the flickering hot flames of a very welcome fire greeted him. In his eagerness to reach the warmth of the fire, he forgot to lower his head to avoid the rafters above and reaped a stunning blow to his skull. He groaned, teetered sickly where he stood for a second or two and then dropped like a falling tree to the wooden floor.

Isla heard the crash of something heavy falling overhead and stilled for an instant. Alissandru must've dropped something or knocked something flying. She rolled her eyes and got on with chopping the vegetables for the stew she was preparing, thinking that at least Alissandru had finally dragged himself out of the shower. The quicker she got the casserole into the oven, the sooner they could eat.

What had Alissandru knocked over? Her brow indented because there was very little clutter in that room and nothing that would make a noise of that magnitude when it fell, unless it was the wardrobe or the chest of drawers. Suddenly anxious, Isla called his name up the stairs and waited but no answer came. Compressing her lips, she went up and through the ajar door saw Alissandru lying in the middle of the floor on his back. He was naked apart from a pair of black cotton boxers. With a stricken exclamation, she sped over to him, horrified to register that he was unconscious. What on earth had he done to himself?

She touched a bare brown shoulder, noting how cold he was, and she jumped to her feet to drag the duvet off the bed and wrap it round him. That small step accomplished, she carefully smoothed her fingers through his hair and felt the smooth stickiness of blood as well as a rising bump. She released her breath in a short hiss and raced back downstairs to lift the phone and call the local doctor.

Unfortunately, the doctor was out attending a home delivery but the doctor's wife, a friendly, practical woman whom Isla had known since childhood, was able to tell her exactly how to treat a patient with concussion and warn her what to expect. Out of breath, she hurried back to Alissandru's side, relieved to see the flicker of his eyelids and the slight movements that signified his return to consciousness.

'Alissandru…?' she murmured.

His outrageously long black eyelashes lifted and he stared at her with a dazed frowning look. 'What happened?'

'You fell. I think you bashed your head on something.'

'Hellish headache,' he conceded, lifting his hand and trying to touch his head. He was noticeably disorientated and clumsy and she grasped his hand before he could touch the swelling.

'Lie still for a moment until you get your bearings,' she urged. 'I'll bring you painkillers when it's safe to leave you.'

Alissandru stared up at her, the blur of her face slowly filling in on detail. He blinked because her hair looked as if it were on fire in the light cast by the flickering flames. Her mop of curls glinted in sugar-maple colours that encompassed every shade from red to tawny to gold. Her blue eyes were full of anxiety and he immediately wanted to soothe her. 'I'm fine,' he told her, instinctively lying. 'Why am I on the floor?'

'You *fell*,' she reminded him again, worried by his confused state of mind. 'Can you move your legs and arms? We want to check that nothing's broken before we try to get you up.'

'Who's *we*?'

'You and me as a team,' Isla rephrased. 'Don't nit-pick, Alissandru. What a fright you gave me when I saw you lying here!'

'Legs and arms fine,' Alissandru confirmed, shifting his lean, powerful body with a groan. 'But my head's killing me.'

'Do you think you could get up? You would be more comfortable in the bed,' she pointed out.

'Of course I can get up,' Alissandru assured her, but it wasn't as easy as he assumed and Isla hoped because the instant Alissandru began to get up, he was overtaken by a bout of dizziness, and Isla struggled to steady him when he swayed.

But he was too heavy for her to hold and he slumped back against the bed for support, shaking his head as though trying to clear it and muttering something in Sicilian that she suspected was a curse. 'I feel like I'm very drunk,' he acknowledged blearily, bracing himself on the mattress to stay upright.

'You'll feel better when you're lying flat again,' Isla declared, hoping she was right while her brain spent an inordinate amount of time struggling to process his near nudity at the same time as guilt that she had noticed that reality attacked her conscience.

But there it was, a near-naked Alissandru was a shockingly eye-catching sight, particularly when Isla had never seen a flesh-and-blood man in that state close up. Of course, she had seen men in trunks at the swimming pool but had never found her gaze tempted to wander or linger on those men, but when it came to Alissandru, dragging her attention from the corrugated expanse of his muscular abs and powerful biceps was a disconcerting challenge. Was it because she knew him? Simple feminine curiosity? Her face burning, she moved forward to help him turn around on unsteady feet and climb into the bed.

But what looked easy turned out to be anything but and in her fear of his falling again she got pinned between him and the bed and safely manoeuvring him down onto the mattress involved a considerable amount of physical contact that drenched her in perspiration and embarrassment. Finally, she managed to get Alissandru lying flat but by that stage she was painfully aware of the tented arousal beneath his boxers that all that sliding against his near-naked bronzed body had provoked. She pounced on the duvet still lying on the floor and flung it back over him with relief.

'No, you lie there and don't move. Don't touch your head either,' she instructed. 'I'm going downstairs to get painkillers for you and the first-aid box.'

Alissandru gave her a dazed half-smile. 'Bossy, aren't you?'

'I'm good in a crisis and this is a crisis because if it hadn't been for Dr McKinney's wife I wouldn't have known what to do with you,' Isla admitted guiltily. 'First chance I get, I'm going to do one of those emergency-first-aid courses that are so popular now.'

'I'll be fine,' Alissandru asserted, unwillingly impressed by her genuine concern for his well-being.

Tania would have kicked him while he was down and taken advantage of his vulnerability any way she could but Isla's only goal was to take care of him to the best of her ability. He rested his aching head on the pillows with a stifled groan, feeling trapped, knowing in frustration that he didn't dare even stand up when his balance was so out of sync. His vision was blurred as well, only slowly achieving normal focus. He should have told her that he had done four years at medical school before his father's death had made his dropping out of university inevitable. Neither his brother nor his mother had been up to the demands of taking control of his father's business enterprises. Alissandru had had to step in and take charge and if, at the time, he had loathed the necessity of giving up his dream of becoming a doctor, he had since learned to love the cut and thrust of the business world and revel in the siren call of new technology worthy of his investment.

Isla returned with a glass of water and a couple of pills. 'Don't know if they'll help,' she said ruefully, trying to prop pillows behind him to help him sit up.

'Might take the edge off it.' Alissandru drained the glass and slumped back down again. 'I want to sleep but I know I shouldn't sleep for long.'

'I didn't know that until the doctor's wife told me that I had to keep checking on you, waking you up if necessary to work out whether you were getting worse. But if the helicopter couldn't pick you up this evening, I'm not sure how the emergency medics could get through either,' she told him ruefully. 'Lift your head.'

Isla knelt beside him, skimming cautious fingers through his luxuriant silky hair and swabbing away the blood, finally spotting the cut and tracing the swelling beneath. 'It doesn't look like it needs stitches but it's still bleeding a little. You could have a fractured skull,' she warned him. 'Try to stay still. I'm going to get dinner into the oven and then I'll come back up.'

'Could you put the light out?' Alissandru asked. 'It's hurting my eyes.'

Isla switched off the bedside lamp and fed the fire to keep it burning. Before she left the room she glanced back at him where he lay in the bed, his dark eyes reflecting the golden heat of the firelight at her. He didn't look right to her lying so still and quiet, his innate restless volatility suppressed.

She finished the casserole and put it on to cook before laying a tray. That achieved, she went up to check on Alissandru. He was awake and watching the fire.

'I'm supposed to ask you stupid questions now like what day it is and who the British Prime Minister is,' she confided.

Alissandru responded straight away with the answers. 'There's nothing wrong with my brain. It's just working slower than usual,' he told her lazily and he stretched out an arm and patted the vacant side of the bed. 'Come and sit down and keep me company. Tell me about you and Paulu.'

Isla went stiff and stayed where she was, belatedly recalling the inheritance he had mentioned and feeling very uncomfortable at the thought of her late brother-in-law having left her anything. 'We were friends. While he and Tania were separated he came to see me several times to talk about her, not that I could tell him much because I didn't know her that well,' she pointed out tautly. 'I liked your brother a lot...but I assure you that there was nothing sexual between us.'

Lifting his tousled head several inches off the pillows, Alissandru shrugged a bare brown shoulder in fluid dismissal. 'It would've explained a great deal if there had been,' he commented.

'There *wasn't*,' Isla emphasised flatly.

'I'm not going to apologise,' Alissandru warned her. 'It was a natural suspicion.'

Isla gritted her teeth, swallowing back a rude remark about his lack of faith in standards of family behaviour and the kind of people he must know to harbour such a sleazy suspicion. He was a hard, distrustful man and she wasn't going to change that reality by arguing with him. 'Paulu would never have been unfaithful to my sister.'

Alissandru compressed his wide sensual mouth. 'More's the pity.'

'I'll bring dinner up when it's ready,' she said stiltedly, burrowing into the hot press on the landing to find fresh clothing for herself and heading into the bathroom for a shower.

She found it *so* hard not to rise to Alissandru's every pointed comment, but she was determined not to lose her temper with him again. It had scared her when she'd lost her temper to the extent she had earlier because she had flown at him like a shrew and tried to slap him. He had brought out a side of her she didn't like. Being that out of control was frightening.

She dried herself on a very damp towel and pulled on her fleece lounging set, which also doubled as pyjamas on the coldest nights. Coloured grey, the set was sexless and unrevealing. In any case, she was convinced that Alissandru's accident had banished any raunchy expectations she might have awakened by succumbing to that kiss. Thankfully they had moved way beyond that level now, she reasoned, scolding herself for the tiny pang of disappointment that made her heart heavy.

She had only once envied her sister, Tania, and that had been when she'd recognised how much Paulu *loved* Tania, regardless of her capriciousness.

Always popular with men, however, Tania had simply accepted her husband's devotion as her due.

But nobody had *ever* loved Isla the way Tania had been loved.

Tania had been the apple of their mother's eye but Isla had barely known the woman and their father had died before she was born. Her grandparents had been both kind and loving but she had always been conscious that she was an extra burden and expense to two pensioners, who had worked hard throughout their lives with very little material reward.

Alissandru's momentary interest had sent Isla's imagination rocketing and made her body fizz with new energy because that kiss had been just about the most exciting thing that had *ever* happened to her. And wasn't *that* in itself a pathetic truth? she told herself with self-loathing.

CHAPTER THREE

WHILE ISLA WAS keeping busy in the kitchen and setting a tray, Alissandru lay back bored in bed and wondered why Isla had yet to ask him *what* she had inherited from his brother. Was that a deliberate avoidance tactic calculated to impress him with her lack of avarice? But why would she want to impress him? After all, regardless of Alissandru's feelings, she *would* receive that inheritance. Her attitude, however, was an anomaly and Alissandru didn't like anomalies. He flatly refused to accept that Tania could have a sister who wasn't greedy. His sister-in-law had craved money the way a dying man would crave water or air.

And moving on from his inflexible conviction that Isla had to be a gold-digger like so many other women he had met, he thought about that kiss and wondered what insanity had possessed him. Tania's sister, *so* inappropriate a choice. But she tasted like strawberries and cream, all the evocative flavours of a summer day and sunlight. Alissandru frowned darkly, forced to recognise afresh that his brain had yet to recover its normal function. That blow to the head had done more damage than he appreciated when his sharp-as-a-tack logic was failing to filter out such a fanciful comparison. Isla was curiously sexy and that was it, no need to be thinking about tastes and flavours, he told himself irritably.

Stupendously sexy, he adjusted, the ready stirring at his groin provoking him to greater honesty. He didn't understand why, he simply recognised that the minute she touched him, or indeed got anywhere near him, he reacted with an almost juvenile instant surge of excitement. A woman had never heated him up so fast or with such ease and it bothered him, because no way was he in the market for an affair with Tania's sister.

Isla brought in the tray, watching as Alissandru dragged himself up against the pillows to accept it. His bronzed skin gleamed in the firelight, accentuating a honed and very muscular physique straight out of a woman's fantasy. Her face burned and she wondered if she should be searching for a pair of her uncle's pyjamas to offer him. But wouldn't that make her look like a prude? It was her bet that Alissandru routinely wore little in bed.

'What on earth are you wearing?' Alissandru enquired as he accepted the tray, his brows drawing together as he studied the furry fabric top and loose bottoms to match.

'It's warm.'

'Where's your meal?' he asked.

'Downstairs,' she admitted stiffly.

'*Per carita*, Isla!' Alissandru exclaimed. 'It's boring up here alone.'

The tip of her tongue slid out to moisten her dry lower lip, discomfiture gripping her. 'I'll bring mine up,' she finally said, feeling a little foolish over her determination to avoid him simply because he made her feel uncomfortable.

She sank down on the side of the bed beside him, both flustered and harassed by the amused glance he flung her as she slowly lifted her legs up after her to balance the tray on her knees. So, it was a *bed*, no need to make a silly fuss about that when there was no chair available, she instructed herself in exasperation.

'You still haven't fully explained your connection with Paulu,' Alissandru remarked softly.

Isla gritted her teeth on her fork. 'We became friends…he was upset about his marriage breaking down and I tried to advise him on how to get Tania back.'

'Good to know who I have to thank for that final mistake,' Alissandru commented drily.

'You need a filter button before you speak,' Isla told him tartly.

'Share with me the advice you gave him,' Alissandru urged.

She turned her head to look at him and, unexpectedly, her heart softened. She recognised the glow of curiosity in his eyes for what it was: a kind of hunger to know and understand *anything* about his twin that he had been excluded from, and naturally Paulu had not shared his eagerness to reclaim his estranged wife with a brother who had probably cheered at her departure.

'Paulu was behaving like a stalker. He was sending Tania emails, texts and showering her with invitations and it wasn't getting him anywhere. Tania was annoyed he had followed her back to London,' Isla admitted ruefully. 'She told me the marriage was over.'

'So, what changed?'

'I don't know for sure because, apart from a text from Paulu telling me they were giving their marriage another go, I didn't get to see either of them again,' Isla confided ruefully. 'But I had warned Paulu to stop chasing her and to back off and give her some space. She took him for granted...you see.'

'*Sì,*' Alissandru agreed grimly.

'But at the same time, Paulu was Tania's security blanket, her safe place, and I suspect that if he did show a little backbone and she started to fear that she truly was losing him for ever, she might think again.'

'It's the eighth wonder of the world that Paulu and I shared the same womb,' Alissandru intoned. 'We barely had a thought in common.'

'You were twins.'

'Fraternal. I inherited more of my father's traits but Paulu didn't have an aggressive bone in his body.'

'He had much more important gifts,' Isla cut in. 'He was kind and loving and generous.'

'*Sì, very* generous,' Alissandru sliced in darkly, setting his tray down and welding his broad shoulders to the headboard in physical emphasis of his exasperated sarcasm. 'If he hadn't almost bankrupted himself *treating* Tania to her every wish before he married her, he wouldn't have got himself into so much financial trouble afterwards.'

Isla set down her tray as well, her heart-shaped face troubled. 'Is that what you always do? Take the gloomy view?'

'The truth can hurt and I don't avoid it,' Alissandru assured her.

'But what you're refusing to see is how *happy* Tania made your brother. You may not have liked her, but *he* adored her and I'm so grateful they got back together before they died,' Isla confessed emotively. 'How happy was he the last time you saw him?'

Unimpressed by her sentimental outlook, Alissandru thought back to his last meeting with his twin. Ironically, only days before the helicopter crash, Paulu had been full of the joys of spring, striding into Alissandru's office to cheerfully announce that Tania was willing to try for a baby. Alissandru had been taken aback by the unashamed depth of his brother's desire to have a child of his own because it was not an aspiration that had ever entered Alissandru's head. No, for Alissandru, having a family featured only in some far distant future and it was not something he felt any need to consider before he even reached his thirtieth birthday.

'He *was* happy,' Alissandru admitted grudgingly, and even as he uttered those words he felt some of the weight of his grief slip free and lighten his heart. Suddenly he realised what a comfort it was to look back and recognise that his twin's last months had been joyful because he had reunited with the love of his life and together they had been planning a more settled future.

Isla turned to study him, her wide blue eyes full of understanding and compassion. 'And doesn't that make *you* feel better? I know it makes me feel better.'

That truth was so simple it positively shrieked at

Alissandru but he had not seen that truth for himself and in a sudden movement he snaked an arm round her and pulled her close.

'*Grazie*...thank you,' he breathed in a hoarse tone of relief, his eyes hot liquid gold with naked emotion.

He had such beautiful eyes, she found herself thinking again, and the spiky black lashes surrounding them only boosted their appeal. And as she gazed up at him he lowered his dark head and crushed her soft mouth under his, sending a wave of such hopeless longing snaking through Isla that she shivered with the effect of it.

'You're cold,' Alissandru assumed, lifting her onto his lap to throw back the duvet and then shift her beneath it and back into his strong arms.

Spontaneous laughter shook Alissandru's body as he held her. 'You feel furry like a teddy bear,' he confided unevenly. 'Is there really a woman underneath the fur?'

Taken aback by both his boldness and his amusement, Isla winced. 'I didn't want to be wearing anything provocative around you.'

'It's definitely not provocative,' Alissandru assured her, long fingers smoothing her soft curls back from her face. 'But then I only need to look at you to want you, *mia bella*.'

Sentenced to stillness by that startling admission, Isla gazed up at him, barely crediting that she was in his arms in a bed. Could it be true that she attracted him to that extent? Even though he had despised her sister and had revealed, with his accusation about Paulu, a worrying bias against her likely character as well?

'Stop thinking so hard,' Alissandru urged her, a fingertip smoothing the frown line forming between her delicate brows.

The heat of his big powerful body filtering through her lounging pyjamas made her feel warm and secure. He actually wanted her. Alissandru Rossetti *wanted* her and somehow that made Isla feel less alone. But then, at the age of twenty-two she had lost every living person who had ever mattered to her and she often felt alone. Her uncle and aunt were one of those couples so content to *be* a couple that they rarely invited visitors and, although they always assured her that she was welcome, Isla was not comfortable inviting herself.

'Are you warm enough now?' Alissandru enquired silkily, a hand sliding beneath her top to splay across her midriff.

Her breath snarled up in her throat at the feel of his big hand against her skin. She couldn't think straight and an instant of panic claimed her because she had never been in such an intimate situation with a man. Her brain whirred at a frantic pace because she knew that Alissandru would expect sex. And why not? another little voice chimed in the back of her head. Why not? *Why shouldn't she?* She was finally with a man who made her heart beat so fast she felt breathless. And shouldn't that be celebrated rather than denied or suppressed?

'Yes…you're as effective as an electric blanket,' she told him awkwardly.

Alissandru dealt her an incredulous look from glittering dark eyes and then his wide sensual mouth curved and he laughed again. 'Never heard that one before.'

And Isla knew it was the moment where she should mention her lack of experience because he obviously hadn't a clue, but pride silenced her. He would think she was a freak still being so innocent at her age and she didn't want him thinking *that* of her, much preferring that he should assume that she was as casual about sex as she had been told he was.

'I feel at peace for the first time in weeks,' Alissandru admitted reflectively. 'What you said about Paulu being happy…it helped.'

'I'm glad,' she whispered, lifting a hand to trace her fingers down over his stubbled jaw line, appreciating the masculine roughness of his skin and the dark shadowing that accentuated his beautifully shaped mouth.

'*Maledizione…ti voglio…* I want you,' Alissandru breathed in a raw, driven undertone, his body hot and taut from even that glancing caress.

His sensual mouth ravished hers, sending a shower of sparks flaring low in her belly, and he shifted against her, letting her feel the hard thrust of his readiness in the cradle of her thighs. The pressure of him at the junction of her thighs electrified her, making her almost painfully aware that that was where she really needed to be touched. He leant back from her to lift her top up over her head and she gasped in surprise, only just resisting the urge to cover her exposed breasts.

The cold air pinched her nipples, and she flushed all over as he gazed down at her hungrily.

'It's a sin to cover those,' Alissandru growled, curving a reverent hand to a lush breast crowned with a pouting pink nipple and dipping his head to savour that peak with his mouth.

Her brain in a wild whirl, Isla felt her back arch of its own volition and her pelvis tilt up as heat surged between her legs. He toyed with her other breast, tugging at the sensitive crest until her head fell back, her neck extending as the storm of her response grew stronger. She had never felt anything so powerful before, had not known her body had the ability to feel anything that intense. And then before she could even catch her breath, Alissandru was divesting her of her pants and prying her thighs apart to bury his wicked mouth there instead.

Shock consumed Isla and she parted dry lips to protest. Of course, she knew what he was doing but it was not something she had ever thought would appeal to her, at least until Alissandru applied his tongue to the most sensitive spot on her entire body and a spectacular wave of sensation engulfed her. And the tide of sensation built and built as he entered her with his fingers until she was writhing in response, agonised gasps torn from her parted lips, and for a split second as that explosive peak of pleasure gripped her she saw stars, jerking and out of control, blissful cries wrenched from her lips.

Alissandru grinned down at her with outrageous satisfaction. 'I love a passionate woman,' he told her thickly. 'You match me every step of the way.'

Isla was in a daze of shattered satiation as he shifted lithely over her and lifted her legs to increase his access to her still-thrumming body. She was reeling with disconcertion at what he had done and what she had felt and even then she was questioning what they were doing when he was supposed to have concussion.

'Do you feel all right?' she asked abruptly.

'In a few minutes I will feel one hell of a lot better,' Alissandru asserted with unquenchable certainty, and she felt the powerful surge of him against her swollen entrance.

There wasn't time for her to tense because he sank into her with raw energy and suddenly he was where she had never felt anyone before and he was thrusting deep and hard. She flung her head back and squeezed her eyes tightly shut as discomfort mutated into a sharp stab of pain but not a whisper of sound escaped her. The instant she registered that the worst was over, her body made her more aware of other sensations, stretching to accommodate his invasion and the deeply satisfying burn of him where she ached for more. And once he set up a fluid rhythm, deep down inside her muscles began to clench and tiny ripples of growing need assailed her.

'You are so tight and hot,' Alissandru growled thickly, dark eyes sheer gold enticement in the firelight casting flickering shadows across the walls and the bed.

Her hips rose to meet his because finally she was part of something, fully involved and sentient and wanting, *wanting* so much she could hardly contain it. The driving need to reach the same plateau again consumed her as he speeded up, his every lithe invasion feeding her hunger while her heart raced insanely fast. The tension inside her knotted and knotted ever tighter until he sent her flying again and the wild excitement and hot, sweet pleasure rolled over her again in wave after wave, leaving her limp and weak as he shuddered over her with his own release.

'That was spectacular,' Alissandru muttered raggedly in the aftermath, rolling off her but carrying her with him and keeping both arms wrapped around her so that she sprawled on top of him, drenched in the hot, already familiar scent of him.

And she had no regrets, Isla recognised in a stark instant of clarity as she pressed her lips sleepily to a broad brown shoulder. Alissandru had made her feel truly *alive* for the first time in months and she felt gloriously relaxed and warm and safe. More troubled thoughts tried to nudge at her but she was far too sleepy to let them in. There would be time enough in the morning to consider what she had done but, just at that moment, she didn't want to torment herself with what she couldn't change.

He was attracted to her but he would never love her. Well, that was life, she told herself drowsily, giving with one hand, taking with the other. It still struck her as better than what she had had before.

She woke up very early and slid out of bed, flinching at the tenderness of her body. She tugged out the case below the bed with care, careful not to make too much noise as she extracted warm clothes to take into the bathroom with her. But she didn't leave the room until she had taken her fill of looking at Alissandru while he slept. His face was roughened with dark stubble, his black hair very dark against the bedding while the long golden sweep of his muscular back was a masculine work of art. Carelessly sprawled across the bed, he looked utterly gorgeous and impossibly sexy. He was out of her league, *totally* out of her league, she told herself as she washed and dressed in the bathroom, hurrying downstairs to let out the dogs and feed the hens.

She would also have to take some hay out to the sheep in their shelter because the snow was probably too deep for them to forage. Wrapped up against the cold, she took care of the livestock first, trudging through the snow to the barn for the hay and driving the old tractor as close to the pasture as she could get so that she could heft the hay into the sheep shelter with greater ease.

By the time she finished her chores, however, her shoulders and back were aching and she was breathing heavily and hoping the snow wouldn't last long because snow made everything twice as much work.

When she walked back indoors, it was an intense relief to shed her outdoor clothing and let her face and hands defrost close to the fire she had banked up the night before, and which she now revived. Steps overhead and the creak of the stairs warned her that Alissandru was about to join her, and she turned her head with a shy smile, not quite sure how to greet him in the light of day and reality. Like a lover? Like a friend? Like a relative? There was no etiquette rule that covered what had taken place between them the night before.

'Isla…' Alissandru came to a halt at the foot of the stairs and studied her, his lean, strong face clenching hard. 'We have to talk.'

'I'll make breakfast,' Isla proffered readily, keen to make herself busy and pretty much unnerved by the grim brooding expression tautening his dark devastating features. He had put his suit back on and, even unshaven, he looked like a super-sleek businessman again, expensive and detached.

'Thank you, but I haven't got time for breakfast… perhaps a coffee?' Alissandru suggested smoothly. 'The helicopter is picking me up in about fifteen minutes. Where were you?'

'Feeding the sheep and the hens,' she explained, putting on the kettle, shaken that he was leaving so immediately while anxiously wondering what he planned to talk about. Puggle was showing a worrying tendency to prowl around Alissandru's feet while growling threateningly and she shooed him away.

Having ignored the dog's ridiculous moves

entirely—for how intimidating did something barely six inches tall think it could be—Alissandru withdrew a folded document from the pocket of his suit jacket, straightened it out and settled it down on the table. 'The details of your inheritance. All you need to do is contact the solicitor and give him your current address and you will receive your bequest. Paulu, I should warn you, also left you his house in Sicily on the family estate…if you are agreeable, I would like to *buy* that back from you as it should stay with my family.'

Isla studied him in dismay, disconcerted that he had plunged straight into the impersonal matter of his brother's will. 'I'll think about that,' she murmured, playing for time, barely able to comprehend the concept of becoming the owner of a property abroad when she had never owned a house before. But she did receive his strong hint that he didn't want her using that house on the Rossetti estate and that made her feel uncomfortable and distinctly rejected.

With hands that shook a little with nerves, she prepared coffee for them both. She had shared a bed with Alissandru last night and that was no big deal in the modern world, she reminded herself firmly. She needed to wise up and expect less. Alissandru only had a few minutes before he had to leave and naturally he would be keen to get the business aspect of Paulu's bequest dealt with first.

'Do you want to discuss the sale of the house now?' Alissandru asked quietly, watching her like a hawk, hopeful she would grab at that option and agree an immediate deal.

For someone dressed like a homeless waif, she contrived to look astonishingly pretty, he acknowledged reluctantly. The cold had forced colour into her cheeks and blown her vibrant hair into a wild curly mop. She fiddled with a stray curl nervously and her sparkling dark blue eyes clung to him. Alissandru studied his coffee instead, keen to move on fast and without fanfare from his monumental error of judgement the night before. He had made a mistake, well, in truth, *several* mistakes, but there was no need to dwell on that unwelcome reality.

'No, let's leave the house aside for the moment,' Isla suggested unevenly, sitting down opposite him. 'I'm sure all that can be dealt with at some more convenient time.'

'Isla…?' Alissandru hesitated. 'Last night was a blunder on my part.'

'A…blunder?' she framed and then paled. 'You mean, a mistake?'

Alissandru lifted his chin in acknowledgement. 'I wasn't playing with a full deck. The concussion and the discussion we had about my brother put me in a weird frame of mind.'

Isla stiffened. 'You kissed me *before* you bashed your head. Are you saying I took advantage of you when you were vulnerable?' she asked in angry mortification.

Dark colour edged Alissandru's high cheekbones and he flung her an incredulous glance. 'Of course not. I'm saying that I was confused and unable to think clearly. Bearing in mind your sister's history with my family, it was very unwise for us to blur those lines with sex.'

Isla was frozen to her chair, feeling very much as though he had punched her in the stomach without warning. He was pairing her with Tania, who was, sadly, dead and buried but also Tania, whom Alissandru had loathed. In fact, he was backtracking so fast from their intimacy it was a wonder he wasn't succumbing to whiplash.

With as much dignity as she could contrive, Isla shifted an offhand shoulder.

'Whatever,' she said as if his about-face meant absolutely nothing to her. 'Do we really need to talk about this?'

Alissandru's lean dark features shadowed and hardened. 'I'm afraid that we do because I didn't take precautions with you. That's what I meant when

I said I was…er…confused. That is an oversight I have never made before and, although I'm quite sure you are on the pill and safe from any risk of pregnancy, I want to assure you that I'm regularly tested and clean,' he completed with icy precision.

Isla could feel the colour draining from her face because the danger of conception or indeed infection had not crossed her mind even once, which seemed to underline how very stupid she had been to impulsively succumb to temptation. The man she had given her virginity to hadn't even noticed her lack of experience and now he chose to simply assume that she was taking contraceptive precautions to facilitate her non-existent sex life with other men. She didn't want to disabuse him on that score because the idea of him worrying that she *could* conceive struck her as even *more* humiliating. And just at that moment, she felt almost overwhelmed by the crushing hurt and humiliation Alissandru was already inflicting on her.

Alissandru was conscious as he watched her turn the colour of the ash scattered on the hearth that he had used all the wrong words because he still couldn't concentrate, couldn't find the words that usually came so easily and smoothly to his lips with a woman. Something about Isla was different and he was different with her too, and that acknowledgement freaked him out.

'I shouldn't think there's much risk of conception from one sexual encounter,' Alissandru asserted confidently, while wondering why she wasn't reassuring him that she was fully protected from such a danger.

'I shouldn't think so,' she mumbled in careful agreement, burning her tongue on the hot gulp of coffee she forced down her clenched throat.

Overhead, the noise of a helicopter intruded, and Alissandru sprang upright with alacrity while Puggle bounced and barked. Alissandru couldn't *wait* to get away from her, Isla interpreted, a sinking sensation of shame over her own conduct gripping her tummy.

'I'll leave my card in case of any…complications,' Alissandru said as he shrugged into his cashmere overcoat at speed and slapped a business card down on the table. 'And the offer for the house will be made in due course. Naturally, it will be a most generous offer.'

Naturally, Isla echoed dizzily inside her head. Only there was nothing natural about anything that had happened between them, she reflected painfully. She didn't believe that waitresses and billionaires regularly got together in the same bed but then what did she know? What did she know about *anything*? she asked herself in sudden anguish, realising that ignorance was anything but bliss when naivety could leave her open to such dreadful humiliation.

'I wish you well in the future,' Alissandru murmured coolly on the doorstep.

And she wanted to bury him deep in a snowdrift, but not before she punched him hard for rejecting her in every way that a woman could be rejected. He had hammered nails of fire into her self-esteem, puncturing her pride on every possible level. But then he wanted to be sure that there was no misunderstanding, wanted to be sure that she would not use his phone number for anything other than the direst emergency.

Alissandru didn't want to *see* her again, didn't want to *talk* to her again, really didn't want *anything* more to do with her at all. Only he had clumsily contrived to put those facts across as politely as he could.

And Isla had no plans to disappoint him, assuring herself that she would sooner be publicly whipped than even glance in his disdainful direction again.

CHAPTER FOUR

ISLA LIFTED THE wand to check it with an unsteady hand. And there it was, what she had most feared to see: the positive pregnancy result that confirmed that she had conceived a child with Alissandru Rossetti. Perspiration beaded her brow and her tummy muscles winced in dismay.

He wouldn't like that news, he wouldn't like that at all, wouldn't be expecting it either if she went by the tone of their final conversation. Of course, he had assumed that she was taking birth-control pills and that the risk of pregnancy would therefore be minimal. Well, he had been wrong and did it really matter how *he* felt about this particular development?

A couple of months ago, following that night they had spent together at the croft, such a discovery would have filled her with sheer panic, Isla acknowledged ruefully, but her life had changed out of all recognition since then. How? Well, first and foremost Paulu Rossetti had left her a very generous amount of money. She was already making plans to sign up at a further education college to remedy the lack of qualifications that restricted her in the job market. She had been forced to drop out of school as a teenager to help care for her grandfather because her grandma hadn't been able to nurse him alone. She had always hoped to go back to school some day to pass the exams she had missed. However, the revelation that she was expecting a child altered everything because even though she could still study while pregnant or as a single mum, her head spun at the amount of organisation it would require and she baulked at the prospect of putting her baby into someone else's care.

After all, Isla very much wanted her baby. In fact, a warm glow spread inside her at the mere thought of the precious burden she carried. Her baby would give her a family again, and wouldn't that be wonderful? Not to be alone any more? To have her child to focus on and look after, to have a seriously good reason for everything she did in the future? And that she could warmly accept its accidental conception was solely down to Paulu Rossetti's generosity and thoughtfulness. Had her sister even known what was in her husband's will? She didn't think it would ever have occurred to Tania to leave her kid sister anything if she passed away first. Of course, Tania had never had much of her own and what she had had she'd spent on designer clothes and the like.

A week after that snowbound night, when Isla had still been feeling very depressed about having slept with Alissandru, her uncle and aunt had returned from New Zealand. After spending a fortnight on the rickety old sofa bed her relatives had borrowed for her use, and catching a bad bout of flu, Isla had been ready to leave. Although she had missed a period by that stage, she had not been unduly concerned because the flu had left her run-down. Only when her menstrual cycle had failed a second time had Isla realised that she needed to buy a pregnancy test, and by then she had flown back to London, encouraged by the fact that her inheritance had given her options. Instead of worrying about where she would stay or how she would afford to stay anywhere without an income, thanks to Paulu she had the luxury of choice. Her friend Lindsay had announced that Isla and Puggle could stay in her flat with her for a while because her flatmate was away on a training course.

Paulu's bequest had included far more money than Isla had ever dreamt of receiving, and no sooner had Isla asked her Scottish solicitor to contact the Rossetti family's solicitor than a ridiculously generous offer had come through to buy Paulu's house back from her. But Isla was, as yet, in no hurry to sell the house and the discovery that Alissandru had got her pregnant had only complicated the situation.

Isla wanted to *see* the house where Paulu and her sister had been living. She wanted to go through Tania's possessions and keep a few sentimental objects to remember her sibling by. And the knowledge that her baby would be a Rossetti had also made her reluctant to immediately sell the house on the family estate. Not that Alissandru would want her there or even visiting, she conceded uncomfortably, but her baby would have rights too, she reasoned, and might well appreciate that connection to his or her Sicilian heritage. No, selling the house, totally breaking that connection, wasn't a decision to be made in haste, she reasoned ruefully…regardless of how Alissandru felt about her owning part of his precious family estate.

So, now what did she do about Alissandru? She would *have* to tell him that she was pregnant because he had the right to know, but she wasn't looking forward to breaking that news because she was convinced that it would be a deeply unwelcome announcement. Alissandru didn't want anything more to do with her, so the news that they would be linked for ever by a child could only infuriate him. But there was nothing she could do about that, so Alissandru would just *have* to deal with it.

Before she could lose her nerve, Isla pulled out her phone and called the number he had given her.

'Alissandru?' she queried the instant she heard his dark deep drawl answer with an impatient edge. 'It's Isla Stewart. I'm sorry to have to bother you but I have something to tell you.'

At the other end of the line, Alissandru had tensed. 'You want more money for the house?' he assumed, stepping away from the conference table he had been seated at, jerking his head in dismissal at his staff as he stalked into his office next door, tension stamped in every angular line and hollow of his darkly handsome features.

'It's nothing to do with the house,' Isla admitted. 'I haven't made a decision about that yet.'

'Why not?' Alissandru cut in edgily.

'Because I've just found out that I'm pregnant and right now that is all I can think about,' Isla confided reluctantly.

A freezing little silence fell at the other end of the line. Alissandru was reeling in silent shock because he had not once considered that possibility and when it came at him out of nowhere, he froze, stunned by her announcement. How *could* she be pregnant? Was it even his? What were the odds?

'I don't understand how this has happened,' Alissandru murmured flatly.

'Well, I've done my duty by telling you and for the moment we can leave it there,' Isla told him, eager to conclude the call. 'We've got nothing to discuss.'

'If what you claim is true we have a great deal to discuss,' Alissandru contradicted harshly.

'Why on earth would I lie about being pregnant?' Isla snapped.

'I don't know, but your sister *did*,' Alissandru told her with ruthless emphasis. 'But be assured that even if you turn out to be having triplets, I'm unlikely to offer a wedding ring.'

Isla sucked in a deep steadying breath. 'Since I'm well aware of your habit of saying exactly what enters your mind and because I have better manners than you have, I will just ignore those comments,' she responded tartly. 'But allow me to assure you that I *am* pregnant, you *are* the father and I wouldn't marry you if you were the last man alive!'

'I will arrange for you to see a doctor first and we will move on from there.'

'I'm ready to move on past you *right now*, Alissandru!' Isla flashed back, so angry she could barely vocalise.

'I will call you back once I've made arrangements,' Alissandru countered grimly and finished the call.

Isla was pregnant? How could that be? Why hadn't the contraceptive pill worked? And why would she have waited weeks to tell him? It seemed like a long time since that night they had spent together. In a rage, Alissandru slammed his phone down on his desk. What an idiot he had been that night to fall into the trap of having unprotected sex! He had run an insane risk and incredibly he had done it with Tania Stewart's sister. Of all the worst possible women to have got entangled with, why had he succumbed to her?

Over the past two months, Alissandru had repeatedly relived that night. Waking or sleeping, he just couldn't seem to shake free of those memories of Isla. The sex had been phenomenal. That was why he couldn't get that night with *her* out of his head. Clearly, he was more driven by his libido than he had ever appreciated and the knowledge that he was guilty of that fatal flaw, that demeaning weakness, had turned him off casual sex and other women. He had not been with a woman since that night, which was probably even unhealthier, he reasoned rawly.

Pregnant! Was it possible? Of course it was possible, but it was equally possible after several weeks that even if Isla *was* pregnant the child would ul-

timately turn out not to be *his* child. Dragging in
a shuddering breath of restraint, Alissandru called
his lawyer to ask for advice and only after that en-
lightening discussion, and in a much cooler frame
of mind, did he organise a medical appointment. He
requested Isla's address by text and informed her that
he would pick her up the next morning at nine and
accompany her to the examination.

Isla gritted her teeth and told him that he would be
waiting outside the door if there was to be any medical examination. She gave him the address, though,
reasoning that once he was satisfied that she was
telling him the truth they could move on and she
would need to have nothing more to do with him.
After all, she didn't need his financial help, did she?
Paulu had left her comfortably off, giving her the
means to raise a child as a single parent. While she
was pregnant, she would attend classes and study,
she decided, making the most of that time before
she sought employment again. Many women were
successful working mothers and so would she be.

Another worry now clawed at her, though. Was it
true that Tania had claimed to be pregnant at some
stage of her relationship with Paulu? Was that, in
fact, why she and Paulu had married as Alissandru
seemed to think? And even if it was true and Tania
had made an understandable mistake in assuming

that she was pregnant when she was not, why was Isla's word now being doubted and why was she expected to hang her head in shame for her sibling's error?

Suddenly, Isla knew exactly what she would be saying to Alissandru in the morning and none of it would be polite, she thought furiously. How could she have slept with a man like that? He was horribly suspicious and distrustful of women. Not to mention unreasonably biased against Isla because of the blood in her veins. She would be the mother of Alissandru's child. How the heck could they ever establish a civilised relationship as parents on that basis? The guy was a living nightmare! Nobody halfway normal could handle him! Her poor sister was dead and he was *still* holding Tania's past actions against her.

Lindsay, a pretty blonde with tough views on men, had an entirely different take on Isla's situation. 'Of course, you need Alissandru's financial help.'

'I don't,' Isla protested.

'Paulu left you a lovely nest egg but it's not going to keep you or a child for the rest of your days. Not unless you flog that house in Sicily as well and invest the proceeds,' Lindsay pronounced. 'And the child is his child, as well…why shouldn't he pay towards his child's upkeep? That's his duty.'

'He assumed I was on the pill.'

'But he didn't ask you if you *were*, did he? You both took the risk and it didn't pay off, so you're not any more responsible for this development than *he* is,' Lindsay completed roundly. 'Stop beating yourself up about it.'

But Isla was tormenting herself because she felt very guilty that on a secret level she was *pleased* to be pregnant and already excitedly looking forward to becoming a first-time mum. Family was what she cared about most and finally she was going to have a family again. At the same time, even the sound of Alissandru's voice on the phone had warned her that *he* was angry, bitter and unhappy about the prospect of her being pregnant with his child. How could she feel anything other than guilty in the circumstances? Another woman might have been willing to consider a termination or adoption but Isla wasn't prepared to consider either of those options.

In the morning, she got up early, ate a good breakfast and donned a winter-weight jersey dress, teaming it with knee-high boots, items recently purchased with her newly affluent bank account. She questioned why she was making that much effort for Alissandru and decided that pure pride was motivating her, because Alissandru had rejected her on every possible level after the night they had spent together. She needed the comfort of knowing she looked her best in Alissandru's radius.

The bell buzzed through the empty flat, Lindsay having long since left for work. Isla used the peephole and undid the chain, standing back as she opened the door. Alissandru stood there, six-feet-plus inches of volatile brooding male.

'Will you come in for a moment?' Isla asked politely.

'The traffic's bad and we don't want to be late.'

'If you want me to go anywhere with you, you have to come in first,' Isla delivered without hesitation, wondering how he could look so gorgeous early in the morning and yet be a total irredeemable toad beneath the surface sophistication.

Wide sensual mouth flattening with annoyance, Alissandru skimmed grim dark golden eyes over the flushed triangle of her face. *Sì*, he reasoned angrily, *already* he could feel the dangerous pull of sexual attraction. The dress cupped the full swell of her magnificent breasts to perfection and hinted at her gloriously curvaceous hips while the boots accentuated legs that were surprisingly long despite her diminutive height. Isla could cover herself from head to toe and screen every atom of bare flesh and still look like a total temptress with her pink sultry mouth, sexy curves and sparkling violet-blue eyes.

She didn't look remotely pregnant to him but then she wouldn't be showing yet, would she? Alissandru knew virtually nothing about pregnancy and at that moment, his ignorance galled him.

'Why do you want me to come in?'

'I want your full attention and I don't want to stage an argument with you while you're trying to drive,' she confided.

'I have a driver,' Alissandru slotted in icily. 'And I do not see what we have to argue about.'

Isla raised a dubious coppery brow. 'Your attitude? It *stinks*. I'm not my sister. I don't look like her and I don't think I behave like her but you can't seem to see that. Getting pregnant after a one-night stand is worrying enough without me feeling that I'm constantly up against your irrational prejudice against me.'

'I do not suffer from irrational prejudice,' Alissandru declared in a stubborn tone of denial.

'Sorry to be the one to tell you but you *do*,' Isla replied quietly. 'I can accept that you didn't like my sister and that it's too late now for you to change your mind about her, but you *have* to accept that I'm a different person. Stop comparing us and being suspicious of my every move because this baby I'm carrying doesn't need that tension in the air between us.'

'Mr Welch will tell us if you *are* carrying a baby

but we won't know if it's mine until the child is born. DNA testing can be done while you are pregnant but it *could* compromise your pregnancy, so I'm prepared to wait for that confirmation until after the birth,' Alissandru informed her, looking very much as if he was expecting a lofty round of applause for that consideration. 'May we leave now?'

'You didn't listen to a word I said, did you?' Isla exclaimed angrily. 'Well, maybe you didn't listen but you can sit down and think about your prejudice later, can't you? I'm tired of dealing with it.'

'The car's waiting,' Alissandru murmured, standing back for her to precede him, careful to be courteous as advised by his lawyer. Arguing with Isla, who was potentially the mother of his child, would be unwise. He needed a plan and then he would deal with the whole situation. *Irrational prejudice?* What was she talking about? She was Tania's sister and naturally he distrusted her. That was *not* unreasonable, he told himself squarely.

The limousine impressed Isla to death but she refused to reveal the fact, sinking into the opulent cream padded upholstery and looking out at the traffic as if she travelled in such style every day. Not a word passed either of their lips until they entered an elegant waiting room to await the appointment he had arranged. When Isla's name was called, an argument broke out when Alissandru stood up, as well.

'No, you can't come in with me. This is private. You can speak to the doctor afterwards with my permission, but you are *not* coming in with me!' Isla warned him furiously, her cheeks infusing with hot colour as the other couple waiting across the room stared at them as though they had escaped from a zoo.

Impervious to such self-consciousness, Alissandru settled glittering dark golden eyes on her. 'I wish to accompany you.'

'I said no, Alissandru, and *no* means *no*!' Isla bit out angrily as she stalked off and left him behind.

Fizzing with pent-up energy and frustration, Alissandru paced the floor. Of course, her pregnancy would be confirmed. He wasn't expecting to discover that she had lied about that, but the real question was whether or not it was *his* child she carried and he wouldn't have the answer to that question for months to come.

Isla found Mr Welch friendly and professional. He confirmed that she was pregnant and seemed a little surprised that she had not experienced any textbook signs of pregnancy like dizziness or nausea. 'Of course, it's very early days,' he added comfortably. 'Now that you know for sure, you'll probably start feeling small effects very soon.'

It was a little embarrassing having to ask the doctor to speak to Alissandru separately, but Isla kept a smile on her face and did so, returning to the waiting room just as Alissandru was called. He was gone for longer than she expected and returned, looking taut and serious, to usher her back out to the limousine.

'So, not a false alarm,' he remarked as the limo moved back into the traffic.

'I'm to come back for a scan in a couple of weeks,' Isla told him brightly, determined not to be affected by Alissandru's mood.

'Do you have any idea why the pills you were on failed?' he asked flatly.

'I wasn't taking any pills,' Isla admitted baldly, keen to get that misunderstanding out of the way. 'You assumed that I was, but I wasn't.'

Alissandru shot her a startled glance. 'In other words, we were entirely unprotected that night.'

Isla nodded stiffly. 'Yes, and I'm as much to blame as you are for not appreciating the risk that we were taking.'

Faint dark colour edged Alissandru's sculpted cheekbones, accentuating the bronzed hollows beneath and the perfect bone structure that gave his face such masculine strength. He was a twin but he and Paulu had not looked much alike, Isla acknowledged. Paulu had been slighter in build and much more boyish in his looks.

'Why weren't you taking any contraceptive precautions?' Alissandru prompted, his wide sensual mouth taking on a sardonic slant.

'I wasn't having sex so there was no need for me to consider precautions,' Isla revealed, lifting her chin, refusing to succumb to her embarrassment. She had had sex with Alissandru, she reminded herself in exasperation. There was no excuse for such prudishness now that she had conceived.

A frown line indented his brow. 'You *weren't*?'

Isla jerked a slight shoulder in a dismissive shrug. 'You were the first…and you didn't notice, but that's all right. To be fair, at the time I didn't want to draw your attention to my lack of experience.'

Alissandru had lost colour below his Mediterranean tan and his stunning dark eyes had narrowed, his black lacelike lashes almost tangling. 'You're telling me that you were a virgin?' he pressed in disbelief.

'Yes, and the sooner you accept that and that this child can *only* be yours, the happier we will both be,' Isla responded doggedly. 'Telling yourself that this child may be someone else's is simply wishful thinking—'

'I refuse to accept that you were a virgin,' Alissandru interrupted in a raw undertone.

Tranquil in that moment as a garden pond, Isla gazed steadily back at him. 'I expected that reaction. You learn everything the hard way. However, I've done what I had to do. I've told you. But I *can't* change the way you think. You can drop me home now and we can talk again after the baby's born.'

Her tone of careless dismissal set Alissandru's perfect teeth on edge. 'Whether the child is mine or not, I will be much more involved before the birth than you seem to expect.'

'I don't think so…not without my agreement. And you won't be getting that. I don't need the aggravation. I want to make plans and look forward to my baby.'

'Look forward?' Alissandru incised thunderously.

Isla gave him a sunny smile, refusing to conceal her feelings. 'Yes, I'm very excited about this baby and I won't pretend otherwise.'

Mindful of his temper, Alissandru breathed in deep and slow. She was delighted to be pregnant, openly admitting it. Was she one of those women he had read about who just decided to have a child and went out and picked a man to do the deed? He gritted his even white teeth. Even if she was, what could he do about it? He was in a situation in which he couldn't win. An unwed pregnant mother held all the aces. He would be damned if he did help her because the child might not be his, and damned if he didn't because if he didn't help her now, he could be denied access after the child was born because his child's mother would hate him.

The child. He remembered how much Paulu had longed for a child, and his heart clenched painfully. Paulu would've celebrated such news and their mother would've been ecstatic at the prospect of a grandchild. Alissandru didn't know how he felt beyond shocked, frustrated and bewildered. He studied Isla from below his lashes, recalling that night in astonishing detail for a person claiming concussion as an excuse for mental confusion. A virgin? He had never been with one. It was true that she had done nothing that implied a higher level of sexual skill. It was also true that he had had to utilise more power than usual to gain access to her squirming little body.

Feeling strangely breathless and hot, Alissandru dragged his smouldering gaze from her and focussed on a leather-clad leg instead. *He had parted those knees.* Hard as a rock and uncomfortable, he shifted position, angling his long, lean, powerful body back into a corner. Yes, it was possible she had been a virgin. Tania's sister a virgin at twenty-two years of age? Surprising but not impossible, he reasoned doggedly, battling his arousal with all his strength.

Isla watched Alissandru, wondering what he was thinking about, wondering if she should even *want* to know. She was on edge in his radius, unable to relax while recalling everything she had worked hard at trying to forget. His touch, the feel of him over her, inside her, the seething, storming excitement of his every movement. He had made her ignite in a blaze of elation and pleasure that still haunted her at weak moments. An ache stirred at the heart of her, warning her that even remembering that night was dangerous. But there he sprawled, effortlessly elegant and infuriating and still breathtakingly beautiful, from the blue-black fall of hair he wore rather longer than was fashionable to the broad shoulders and powerful muscular torso that even the fanciest suit couldn't conceal.

'We could talk over an early lunch at my town house,' Alissandru suggested, startling her out of her reverie.

'I don't think we have anything to talk about at present,' Isla said in surprise.

'That's where you're wrong,' Alissandru asserted without hesitation.

'I wish I could say that that declaration surprises me…but I can't,' Isla said ruefully. 'You always think you're right.'

CHAPTER FIVE

ALISSANDRU'S TOWN HOUSE lay off a quiet, elegant Georgian square. It was a family-sized house, not at all the ritzy single-man accommodation Isla would have expected him to inhabit and, when she commented, he confided that he needed a spacious property because his family stayed with him when they were visiting London.

'My mother likes London for shopping and so do my cousins. She usually brings company with her.'

An inner shudder of recoil assailed Isla as she recalled Alissandru's cousin Fantino, who had cornered her in that bedroom in Sicily and assaulted her. Not that she had recognised it as an actual assault at the time, being young and ignorant of such labels. Tania, after all, had dismissed the incident as a misunderstanding and had angrily warned a distraught Isla not to kick up a fuss over what had happened and spoil her wedding day. Did Fantino come to London? Was Alissandru close to him? The men were about the same age. Suppressing her wandering thoughts, she pushed the matter and that unfortunate connection back out of her mind again.

Alissandru showed her into a contemporary dining room decorated in fashionable shades of soft grey and tucked her into a comfortable chair. 'Would you like a drink?' he enquired.

'No, thanks. Alcohol is off my menu for the immediate future—better safe than sorry,' she quipped.

'I didn't know. In fact, I don't know anything about pregnant women apart from the fact that they put on weight and get very tired,' Alissandru admitted wryly. 'And I only picked up that from listening to my cousins' complaints.'

His honesty disconcerted her. She watched as an older woman brought in a tray and set plates out for them. It was a light meal, exactly what she preferred at present because, although she had yet to feel sick, her appetite had dwindled and she had lost a little weight.

'You said that we had to talk,' she reminded him as she sipped at her water. 'What about?'

'About me getting involved in all this,' Alissandru specified. 'You're behaving as if you want me to step back and stay out of things until after the birth.'

Isla glanced up, her violet eyes troubled. 'That *is* what I want.'

'That won't work for me,' Alissandru countered bluntly. 'I'm opening a bank account for you to take care of your expenses. Who are you living with at present?'

Isla flung back her shoulders. 'A friend, but it's only a temporary arrangement. I'll need to find my own place. Alissandru… I really don't need your financial help, not when I have what Paulu gave me.'

'I *have* to contribute,' Alissandru spelt out resolutely.

'Even though you're not convinced that this is your child?' Isla snapped in exasperation.

'Even though,' Alissandru confirmed without hesitation. 'I also intend to cover all your medical expenses and, with your agreement, accompany you to any important procedures…such as the scan Mr Welch mentioned was coming up. You can't ask me to stand back and act like this has nothing to do with me. If this is my child I need to take an interest and take responsibility, as well.'

Isla swallowed hard on the flood of disagreement rising to her lips. Alissandru was very much a man of action and she could hardly fault him for stepping up to demand a share of the responsibility. He didn't want to be excluded. He didn't want to stand on the sidelines hearing stuff third-hand from her. But his wish to get involved contravened her earnest need to shut him out. Not very charitable, she scolded herself, not very fair. He had rejected her but he was not rejecting the possibility of their child. He was trying to do the right thing and if she denied him, it would only increase his distrust.

Playing for time, Isla toyed with her food. 'I understand what you're saying but I don't need your money.'

'Allow me to contribute towards your expenses. I want you to have the very best medical care and decent accommodation. I don't want you worrying about the future.' Brilliant dark golden eyes rested on her. 'I *must* help. That's not negotiable. I need to be supportive. I won't interfere in your life, but I will be there in the background.'

Somewhat soothed by that reference to his staying in the background, Isla sighed. 'I suppose I can hardly say no. I will keep you informed but I don't want anything else to do with you. I don't think that you can expect any warmer welcome from me after the way we parted in Scotland.'

'I don't want to upset you in any way,' Alissandru told her. 'But I do need to be part of this situation.'

Travelling back to the office, having dropped Isla home, Alissandru took stock at a more leisurely and reflective pace than was usual for him. He was imbued with the energetic conviction that he had plans to make, a *lot* of plans. First and foremost, he needed to find somewhere comfortable and with good security for Isla to live because at present she wasn't staying in one of the safest areas of the city. Where she lived was a priority, he reasoned. And Mr Welch had impressed on him that she also needed a healthy diet so he would organise some sort of food service or delivery, as well.

A baby. If it was a little boy, it might be a little like Paulu, he reasoned, startling himself with that thought. Or why not a little girl with Paulu's sweet nature? He didn't care either way and his mother would be ecstatic with either possibility, for Constantia Rossetti was still struggling to cope with the loss of her son. A baby would be something positive to focus on and ultimately a comfort to them all.

As long as it was *his* child…

But why would Isla lie on that score? He had warned her that he wouldn't marry her because naturally he couldn't forget the disaster of his twin's hasty marriage with Tania. Tania had wanted a rich husband much more than she had ever wanted a child. Isla, on the other hand, needed persuasion before she would even accept Alissandru's involvement and financial support during her pregnancy. She hadn't snatched at his offer for Paulu's house, either.

Maybe she was playing a long game and trying to impress him, although it was hard to see what she could gain from denying her legal right to have his support. Maybe he *was* too jaded after Paulu's experience to see the wood for the trees, he conceded uneasily, frowning at the mere suspicion that he could deserve Isla's accusation of irrational prejudice. Regardless, however, he was already beginning to see a much more positive angle to the baby scenario.

His interest had been caught, and was that thanks to Paulu, as well?

'What's it all for?' his twin had demanded that day in Alissandru's office when he'd admitted his own desire for a child. 'Who have you built this empire for? You already have more than you could spend in a lifetime. Wouldn't you like a son or daughter to leave it all to?'

And Alissandru had laughed, deeming that a question for the future, not the present, only now everything had changed and it was amazing how priorities could rearrange themselves in the aftermath of loss. Paulu was gone and there was nothing he could do about that, but a child would give him a fresh focus. A child would need teaching and guidance and love. Alissandru suddenly smiled at the prospect. A baby just might be exactly what he needed...

* * *

Two days later, Isla lay in bed mulling over her final conversation with the father of her child. It wasn't so much that Alissandru wanted to be part of the situation, more like he wanted to *take over*. He had already sent her details of three London properties he owned, inviting her to move into any one of them at his expense but, although it was a very lavish offer, Isla didn't want to become Alissandru Rossetti's kept woman. At the same time she only had a week to find somewhere of her own to live because Lindsay's flatmate would be returning soon. It would be easier to accept Alissandru's offer but the easy way wasn't always the wisest way, Isla acknowledged uneasily.

But she *knew* that the child she was carrying was *his* child even if he did not and it would not be as though she would be taking advantage of his generosity. He had also organised an early scan for her with Mr Welch and she had wanted to turn down that offer too, but she was too eager to see her baby for the first time, even if it was only the size of a pea. Alissandru also knew how to tempt a woman, she conceded ruefully, but could she face a scan at which he would undoubtedly expect to be present, as well? she asked herself. She would only be baring her stomach...

In the early hours of the following morning, Isla

wakened to a cramping pain that made her wince. She sat up in bed, a sensation of dampness between her thighs stirring anxiety. When she realised that she was bleeding she started to panic. Was she losing her baby? What had she done wrong? Hadn't she looked after herself well enough?

Lindsay calmed her down and rang the emergency helpline, herding Isla into clothes and then into a taxi to take her to hospital. Her friend told her all sorts of soothing stories about false alarms and minor complications and Isla managed to hold herself together while they sat for hours waiting their turn in the hospital waiting room, surrounded by a mass of other anxious people.

In the end it took very little time for her to be dealt with. A doctor told her gently that if she was suffering a miscarriage nothing could be done to stop it happening and that such an experience was much more common than she realised in early pregnancy. Isla sat frozen to her seat as if a sudden movement might provoke a more serious crisis. Ushered into another room, she was prepared for a scan by a radiographer. Suddenly the kind of scan she had earlier been so much looking forward to receiving harboured a more menacing vibe.

The wand moved smoothly over her still-flat tummy, and Isla was barely breathing as she strained without success to see something recognisable as a baby on the screen. When the woman stopped and reached for her hand, Isla knew what was coming because the radiographer looked so sad for her.

'I'm so sorry. There's no heartbeat. It's not a viable pregnancy,' she said quietly.

A junior doctor saw her next. Isla was in shock: her baby was dead. Her wonderful beautiful baby was gone as if it had never been. Her surroundings suddenly seemed to be stretching away from her and she couldn't concentrate on what was being said. The doctor pressed medication into Isla's limp hand while Lindsay sat beside her not even trying to hide her tears, but Isla couldn't cry. Her eyes stayed dry while a great gulping sob of anguish seemed to be trapped somewhere in her throat, making it a challenge to breathe or speak.

'I'm so sorry,' Lindsay whispered in the taxi on the way back to the flat. 'This has happened to a couple of my friends at work. It's why some women won't tell anyone that they're pregnant until they're past the first trimester. That's the danger period...'

Isla nodded vigorously, striving to be strong and stoic, reluctant to subject her friends to the tears penned up inside her. 'It could have been the flu I had,' she mumbled.

'It could have been any of a dozen things.' Lindsay sighed. 'Do you want to talk about it?'

But, suddenly, Isla felt that there was nothing left to talk about. Talking wasn't going to bring her baby back and she had already kept Lindsay out of bed for half the night, she reflected guiltily. Her poor friend still had to go into work in the morning and she was already exhausted. Assuring Lindsay that all she wanted to do was sleep, she went back into the bedroom. Her first real thought was that she would have to tell Alissandru and that he would be pleased. Not that he would dare to *say* it, she assumed bitterly, but he had seen their baby as an undesirable complication and now that their baby was no longer on the way, he could only be relieved.

Unfortunately, Isla wasn't relieved because the whole cosy future she had envisaged around that precious baby had suddenly been cruelly taken from her and she didn't know what to do next. That was scary when she had felt so confident about managing everything after she first realised that she was pregnant. Now the floor of her world had suddenly vanished and she was fighting just to stay afloat.

The next morning, she agonised at length over the need to contact Alissandru. She couldn't face phoning him, saying those wounding words out loud about her baby and, midmorning, she sent him a text bluntly telling him that she had had a miscarriage.

In receipt of that unexpected message, Alissandru stared at his phone and felt sick. A *miscarriage*? How had that happened? Suddenly he was full of anxious questions.

'Something wrong?' one of his directors asked, and Alissandru glanced up, only then registering that his companions were regarding him expectantly.

'I've had bad news,' Alissandru admitted soberly. 'If you will excuse me...'

Isla's news had blindsided him even more than the announcement that she was pregnant. One minute they were having a baby, the next...? It was dead. He stared out of his office window, fighting the feelings engulfing him just as he had fought them when he'd learned that Paulu had died. He had to be strong, he *always* had to be strong because other people relied on him to be that way. When it had been Paulu, his mother had needed him, but now Isla needed him more because Isla had *wanted* that baby. *Their* baby, he adjusted, reluctant to credit any other option in that moment. He remembered Isla's glorious smile as she'd admitted how much she was looking forward to becoming a mother and he lost colour, his eyes prickling. She *had* to be devastated. He rang her immediately.

'Isla, it's Alissandru.'

'I've got nothing to say to you,' she framed woodenly.

'I got your text and obviously I want to see you and talk to you. I'm very sorry.'

'Are you?' she questioned doubtfully.

Anger flared in Alissandru's dark golden gaze. 'Of course I am! I'd like to come round and talk to you.'

'No, thanks,' she cut in immediately. 'I don't want to see you.'

'Have you had proper medical treatment?' Alissandru asked worriedly.

'Yes. I'll be fine,' she told him stiffly.

'Obviously, it wasn't meant to be,' Alissandru said heavily, raking long fingers through his tousled black hair in a gesture of frustration because he honestly didn't know what else to say to her. Words were empty. Words wouldn't change anything. He didn't want to mutter meaningless platitudes the way people did when they were faced with a difficult situation, nor did he feel that he could dare admit that he was upset, as well. Because she would *never* believe him, never believe that he too was full of regret for what was not to be.

He had warmed up to the idea of the baby just a little *too* late, he acknowledged grimly. The baby had been a surprise and he wasn't good with surprises.

He had never liked the natural order and routine of his life being changed or threatened. Predictably the advent of a baby would have altered many things and he had resisted that prospect to the best of his ability, until he'd defrosted enough to concede that a baby could just be the best thing that had ever happened to him.

It wasn't meant to be... Isla flinched from that crass and demoralising assurance that cut to the quick. No, in Alissandru's rarefied world, billionaires did not have babies with former waitresses. Now, mercifully for him, if not for her, the real world had intervened, and no such baby would be born and the status quo would be preserved. Of course, he was relieved and fatalistic about her miscarriage. He hadn't wanted their baby in the first place, could hardly be expected to cry crocodile tears now that there was no longer a baby to worry about. Unlike her he hadn't learned to love their child, hadn't even begun to accept that the baby she carried *was* his child.

A bitterness as cutting as a knife slashed painfully through Isla and she finished the call. Without even thinking about it, she blocked Alissandru's number on her phone because she didn't want to be forced to speak to him again, *ever* again. That connection was finished for ever, severed by fate. She would never have to see him again, never have to speak to him again, never be hurt by him again. Eyes wet, she discovered that that was no comfort whatsoever.

The following morning, Lindsay got a call from her parents and grimaced through the conversation while offering repeated apologies for being unable to change her own plans.

'What's wrong?' Isla prompted.

Lindsay grimaced. 'My parents' friends are going on a round-the-world trip and they had a house-sitter organised to look after their pets. Now the house-sitter has cancelled and Mum and Dad are trying to put together a group of us to look after their house and their animals. I feel awful for saying no but I'm not prepared to use up my leave sitting in the back of beyond looking after dogs and cats,' she confided guiltily.

Isla, petting Puggle, who was turning into a lap-dog, given to sleeping across her feet and nestling in her lap at every given opportunity, looked thoughtful. 'Could *I* do it? The house-sitting, I mean?'

'You?' Lindsay queried in surprise.

'Well, if I could bring Puggle with me, I'd be glad to get away for a while. I mean, I have to find somewhere to live anyway and the change, a little breathing space, would do me good while I decide what to do next.'

Lindsay frowned thoughtfully and warned Isla

that her parents' friends lived in a converted farm-house down a long track in Somerset and that it was a very quiet area. After a few minutes, however, she called her parents back and before Isla could even catch her breath it was all arranged and she was agreeing to travel to Somerset at the end of the week to meet the Wetherby family and receive their instructions before they departed. Isla breathed easier at the prospect of leaving London and Alissandru far behind her. A change of scene and the time and space to make practical plans were exactly what she needed, she told herself urgently.

It wasn't meant to be... His words haunted her but where Alissandru was concerned there were no sad thoughts of what might've been in Isla's troubled mind. His rejection had been brutal and blunt. She had been a mistake, a mistake he regretted, and the miscarriage and his reaction to it had drawn a final line under that reality.

And yet she had been drawn to Alissandru Rossetti in a way she had been drawn to no other man. That bothered her, seriously bothered her. Admittedly he was gorgeous but she had been aware of his prejudice from the outset and should've protected herself better, holding back instead of surrendering to the fierce attraction between them. She had believed that she could be totally adult and blasé about sleeping with him and she had been devastatingly wrong in that assumption because Alissandru had ultimately hurt her more deeply than anyone had ever hurt her. She was not as tough as she had believed and was now even more painfully aware that she had to get tougher.

When Alissandru turned up that evening, Lindsay tried to head him off, but when he became icily imperious with her unfortunate friend, Isla gave up listening behind her bedroom door and emerged, bitterly conscious that she looked a mess.

'Alissandru…' she said flatly.

He had never seen her so pale, her freckles stark across her porcelain skin, her violet eyes dull and haunted. He had to tighten his hands into fists not to reach for her, not to try to offer the physical comfort that he knew would be offensive to her. 'I don't want to crowd you, but I thought you might want to talk,' he reasoned quietly.

Bitterness flashed through Isla, sharp and painful and unfamiliar, for such bitterness did not come naturally to her. 'We have nothing left to talk about,' she told him curtly.

Alissandru looked amazing…*of course* he did, breathtakingly elegant in a dark designer suit that was exquisitely tailored to his lean, muscular physique. He emanated energy and authority in vibrant waves, the smooth planes of his high cheekbones taut below his incredibly expressive dark golden eyes. Such stunning eyes, now telegraphing the kind of guilt that was unwanted because she knew as well as he knew that he hadn't wanted their baby and that any offer of sympathy was sheer hypocrisy on his part. Yet the sheer pulsing zing of his dark, sizzling, sensual allure still filtered through that awareness, mocking her failing self-discipline as every skin cell in her body fired with wanton renewed energy.

'Why don't we have dinner and discuss that?' Alissandru murmured hoarsely, his tension increasing as she stood there, her delicate face colouring with much-needed warmth, lighting up her sad eyes and accentuating her fragility.

'I'm leaving London in a couple of days, so there'd be no point,' she declared. 'I'll let you know what I decide to do about Paulu's house once I've thought stuff over.'

Alissandru was startled by the truth that he had genuinely forgotten about the house. 'I'm not such a bastard that I'd trouble you with that matter *now*,' he argued in a vehement undertone. 'Where are you going to stay?' he pressed curtly.

'That's my business,' Isla assured him, half closing the door. 'Goodnight, Alissandru.'

Where the hell was she going? Would she be safe

there? Would someone be looking out for her? Looking after her? She looked like hell! With difficulty, Alissandru suppressed his concern, acknowledging that it was time for him to move on. He could hardly force Isla to talk to him or to listen to him. He had walked away from her in Scotland and now he had to do it again. He could not understand the wrenching sense of loss attacking him or the sensation that something in his world was very wrong. 'I'll stay in touch,' he breathed in a driven conclusion.

Good luck with that, Isla thought wryly, knowing she was not about to unblock his number on her phone. Alissandru Rossetti was in the past now and only wounding memories would result from any further contact from him. She had to find a new focus in life, she told herself urgently, and embrace her future alone.

CHAPTER SIX

ISLA EXPERIENCED JOY for the first time in many weeks when she first saw the glorious cherry trees that lined the imposing private road that led up to the Palazzo Leonardo. Great foaming swathes of white blossom hung low above her hire car, making her feel as though she were driving through a tunnel of bridal lace.

It was a hot day, hotter than she had naively expected in spring, and she recognised familiar sights in every direction she looked on Rossetti land. Her visit at the age of sixteen had filled her with more memories than she had ever cared to recall. Although it had been her only trip abroad, Fantino's assault had distressed her and made her reluctant to dwell on her recollections of her visit to Sicily.

The Rossetti family lived in a very grand home but the place where their ancestors had chosen to build was quite simply magnificent. A lush green grove of natural woodland covered the hills behind the ancient *palazzo*, which presided over a wonderful patchwork carpet of lemon and orange groves, olive trees and vines. It was still very much a working agricultural estate, and Paulu had run the estate for his brother.

Stiff with considerable nervous tension, Isla parked on the gravel fronting the sprawling property. She had to call at the *palazzo* to pick up keys and directions for Paulu and Tania's house but it would only be polite to greet Paulu's mother first and offer her her condolences and some explanation for her arrival. Constantia Rossetti had been very kind to Isla when she had attended her son's wedding and, since Isla was planning to live in Paulu and Tania's home for at least a few weeks, she wanted to be on good terms with the older woman.

As far as Isla had been able to establish, Alissandru was still in London. The fact that she had lost Alissandru's child or that they had ever got close enough to even conceive a child was a secret, she thought gratefully, a secret known only to the two of them. Not that Alissandru had been grieving, she conceded ruefully. An Internet search of his recent activities had shown him attending a charity function with a beautiful but severely underdressed blonde on his arm. Was that sort of woman the type he went for? Skinny as a twig and showing off all of her flat chest?

Clutching a wriggling Puggle tightly beneath one arm, for Isla did not dare to leave him unattended in the hire car when he was still so disposed towards chewing anything within reach, Isla hit the modern doorbell. The bell was somewhat comically over-shadowed by the giant wooded metal-studded dou-ble front doors that provided the main access to the *palazzo*.

A manservant greeted her and without hesita-tion showed her through the echoing main hall out into the delightfully feminine orangery, which was decorated in classic pale colours. The entire wall of glass, which overlooked a courtyard garden, had been pushed back to al[...] fresh air and sun-shine from outside t[...] [...]ate indoors. The single occupant, a tall dignified woman with greying hair swept up in a chignon, stood up with a quiet smile.

'Isla… I can hardly believe that you're here with us again,' she remarked warmly.

'I'm so sorry that it's taken me this long to visit,' Isla murmured, offering her condolences and a brief explanation for her failure to attend the funerals. 'But I wanted to see the house.'

'Of course, you did,' Constantia commented sympathetically. 'I haven't been back since…er, the crash, although I have ensured that the house was kept clean. Nothing has been touched or changed.

I want you to know that. Everything is exactly as it was when they left that morning.'

'I'll go through my sister's stuff,' Isla proffered hurriedly. 'And perhaps Alissandru would like to take care of his brother's things when I've left again?'

'Is this only a flying visit?' the older woman asked as a tray of tea was brought into the orangery, and in response to her inviting gesture Isla took the seat beside hers, feeling ridiculously like a schoolgirl in the older woman's dignified presence.

'I'm afraid I don't know. I haven't made up my mind about what I'm going to do next,' Isla told her, her cheeks warming a little with self-consciousness as she thought of the short-lived secret interlude she had had with Alissandru.

'Oh, what a dear little dog!' Constantia carolled, stroking Puggle beneath his chin and urging Isla to let him down to explore while she explained that her pug had died the previous winter and she had not yet had the heart to replace him.

The older woman was friendly and welcoming, although tears were visible in her eyes more than once as she reminisced about her son, finally squeezing Isla's hand and apologising for her emotionalism by saying, 'It's such a treat to talk about him to someone.'

'But don't you and Alissandru talk?' Isla had asked before she could think better of that personal question.

'Alissandru doesn't like to discuss such things,' his mother admitted wryly.

Puggle scrambled up onto Constantia's lap with the insouciance of a dog who knew how important humans were to his comfort. Fed crumbs of chocolate cake, he quite naturally refused to get down again, and when the older woman offered to look after him for Isla, to let her get established at the house and do some shopping, Isla didn't have the heart to take him away again when she could see that Puggle's easy affection was a comfort to her hostess.

An estate worker called Giovanni was summoned to guide her to the house, which Paulu had extended and modernised to please her si......d initially described the property as a 'horrible, dark, dank, cobwebby hole of a place'. There wasn't even a hint of darkness about the building slumbering in the warmth of midmorning, brilliant sunlight reflecting off the sparkling windows and accentuating the cheerful yellow shutters and the plant pots that sat around the front door. It looked so peaceful that it made Isla's heart ache when she reflected that the house's previous owners would never live there again.

Scolding herself for that sad thought, she let herself into the hall and then froze in the porch doorway at the sight of a little stool covered with leopard-print fur fabric and dripping with cerise crystal beads. It was outré, ridiculous, very, very much to her flamboyant sister's taste, and she knew she would never part with it yet it was so out of keeping with Paulu's murderously tidy and conservatively furnished and decorated study. Two very different people, Isla acknowledged, and yet in the end they had made their relationship work with both of them making compromises to achieve a better fit.

Tania must've loved him, Isla decided, seeing no other reason for her sister to agree to live in a quiet country house far from the more sophisticated amusements she enjoyed. Her eyes wet with tears, she walked through the house, peering into cupboards and standing feeling like an intruder in doorways. Everywhere she spotted flashes of her extrovert sister's personality. It was there in the bright colours, the marital bedroom awash in cerise pink and white lace like the ultra-feminine lair of some cartoon princess. She closed the door on that room, telling herself that she would start going through stuff in the morning while choosing a guest room for her own occupation. The room was still furnished with antiques and it had plain whitewashed walls. It had always been the estate manager's house, Paulu had once told her, and presumably that was one good reason why Alissandru wanted it back again. Obviously he had to have a property to offer to his twin's replacement.

She supposed her only real option was to sell the house back to Alissandru. If she hoped to buy a house in England she would have to sell, and maintaining a second home abroad would be far too expensive. Even so, that didn't mean she couldn't first enjoy a few weeks vacationing in Sicily on a beautiful private estate. Alissandru wouldn't like her being here in *his* brother's house on *Rossetti* land, though… well, what was that to her now and why should she care that she was an unwelcome visitor?

Her thoughts were interrupted by the arrival of one of the *palazzo* staff laden with food to fill her empty fridge, and they even prepared a meal for the evening, sparing her the pressure of having to go on an immediate shopping trip. Isla smiled, charmed by Constantia's welcoming kindness. At least she didn't have to worry about how Alissandru's mother felt about her arrival.

Almost two months spent mostly alone in a comfortable old farmhouse had gone a long way towards restoring Isla's peace of mind. Walking dogs and feeding kittens had kept her fully occupied. She would never forget the baby she had lost, but that first punishing weight of grief had eased. Worrying about what to cook for her next meal had been the summit of her problems in Somerset, but even there she had become disturbingly aware that she still harboured a great deal of anger and bitterness towards Alissandru. That was *why* she couldn't forget him, that was why she had regularly scoured the Internet for references to him, gleaning facts and figures and a list of glittering business triumphs, all of which had utterly failed to shade in the nuances of his complex and volatile character.

After an early evening meal, she ran a bath for herself and borrowed a silk robe from Tania's wardrobe because she had neglected to pack one. After she had bathed she would drive back up to the *palazzo* to collect Puggle, who would surely have worn out his welcome by then or eaten his way out of house and home. Always hungry, he was a greedy little monster of a dog for all his small size, she acknowledged ruefully as she settled into the deliciously warm water.

She was drifting close to falling asleep in the cooling water when she heard the loud knocking on the front door, and with a groan she sat up, water sloshing noisily around her. Who on earth could it be? Had Constantia sent someone down with Puggle? Roughly towelling her dripping body only semi-dry, she grabbed up the robe and threw it on, grimacing as it clung to the damp parts she had missed with the towel. Barefoot, she sped down the wooden stairs.

Alissandru was in an ungovernable rage. He had flown home unexpectedly, walked into his own home and had been unceremoniously bitten by a nasty little animal he had believed to be hundreds of miles away in another country. As his mother had cooingly picked up the vicious little brute to check that he had not hurt his teeth, Alissandru had been fit to be tied but his brain had been firing on all cylinders in shock that Isla could actually be in Sicily, in his brother's house, on *his* estate.

And that startling, baffling revelation had enraged Alissandru, who liked everything spelled out in clear black-and-white predictable terms. Isla had *refused* to see him, *refused* to speak to him, refused even to take his phone calls, and yet without even giving him a warning she could take up residence in Paulu and Tania's house barely a quarter of a kilometre from him. How was he supposed to feel about that? Obviously they were going to see each other on the estate and was she planning to flaunt her hostile attitude to him here at his home? Was this why she hadn't agreed to sell the house? Had she always planned to show up in Sicily and make his life uncomfortable?

Her hand closing the lapels of the iridescent robe as it tried to slide open at her throat, Isla opened the door. 'Sorry, I was in the bath,' she began breathlessly before she saw who it was. Typically, Alissandru was sheathed in a tailored black suit that only emphasised his towering height and broad, muscular build.

In a maddening instant, Alissandru was confronted head-on by everything he had tried to forget about Isla: the triangular face dominated by huge dark blue eyes, her vivid mop of tousled curls springing back from her pale brow in a contrast that intensified the porcelain clarity of her skin. For Alissandru it was as though everyone else he met was depicted in monotone grey and only Isla was shown in full colour. Even worse, for the first time ever he was seeing her scantily clad and the idea that anyone else might have witnessed how the thin fabric of her robe clung wantonly to her voluptuous curves incensed him. He could see her nipples, the slenderness of her waist, the pronounced curve of her hips, and the hardening swell of arousal at his groin was painfully familiar.

'Alissandru…' Isla framed stiltedly, staring out at him wide-eyed as though he had risen cloven-

hooved and fork-tailed out of the cobblestones behind him, her heart jumping behind her breastbone
in shock.

And yet she had *known* she would see Alissandru, had known they could hardly avoid each other
on his family estate and that her arrival would infuriate him. The golden blaze of his eyes, so bright in
his lean, darkly devastating face alerted her to his
mood and she took a cautious step back. 'I thought
you'd still be in London.'

'I always come home now at weekends if I can,'
Alissandru admitted. '*Per l'amor di Dio*...what are
you doing here?'

In receipt of that question, a little inner devil
overpowered Isla's caution. 'I have every right to
be here. This is *my* house,' she pointed out, lifting
her chin.

Alissandru compressed his beautifully shaped
mouth. 'It is, but you know that I wish to buy it
from you.'

Daringly, Isla turned on her heel, turning her back
on him while leaving the door open because she was
determined not to politely invite him in. 'I don't owe
you any explanations about why I'm here.'

Behind her she heard the front door snapping shut.
'Did I say that you did?' Alissandru growled like a
grizzly bear.

'If I give you enough rope, you'll soon hang your-self,' Isla forecast witheringly. 'I know you don't want me here.'

'When did I ever say that?' Alissandru demanded, following her into the open-plan lounge with its sunken seated area and flashy built-in bar topped by a glittering disco ball, which was so out of place with the rest of the house.

Isla flipped round, her robe flying momentarily open to reveal a sleek stretch of pale pink inner thigh and a slender shapely knee. His mouth ran dry at the sight while he recalled the satin-soft smooth-ness of her skin.

Isla frowned, hating the way he was staring at her. 'You didn't need to say it after you made it clear that you didn't want anyone outside your family owning any part of this estate.'

'I won't apologise for that conviction,' Alissandru argued in frustration as he squared up to her, wide shoulders thrown back, long, powerful legs braced. 'The estate depends on the properties we own. We house our employees. Your ownership could lead to all sorts of complications. You could decide to rent it out, bring in strangers, turn it into some kind of business, argue about rights of way.'

Unimpressed by that parade of evidently dire pos-sibilities, Isla folded her arms and stared back at him.

'I'm not planning to do any of those things… *Satisfied?*' she prompted.

'You know that's not what I'm trying to say.'

'I just want you…*gone!*' Isla surprised herself by throwing out her arms in angry emphasis of that fervent wish.

'Couldn't you have warned me that you were intending to come here?' Alissandru demanded imperiously. 'Or would that common courtesy have crossed the line that says I have to be the bad guy in your every scenario?'

Isla gazed back at him, her attention locked to his lean, strong features and the raw tension stamped in the set angle of his jawline, the flare of his nostrils and the anger smouldering like an unquenchable fire in his stunning eyes. 'Well, you pretty much are the bad guy in every scenario…and let's not pretend that you make much effort to be anything else!' Isla slammed back at him furiously.

Alissandru froze as though she had slapped him, colour leaching from below his bronzed skin. 'You're talking about the baby, aren't you?' he prompted curtly.

Isla barely knew what she was talking about but that very personal question knocked her back on her heels and she rested disconcerted eyes on him. 'No, I'm not, I'm really not.'

'What else am I to think when you say I'm the bad guy in every situation?' Alissandru pressed between clenched teeth.

'Well, when aren't you the bad guy?' Isla demanded. 'You were certainly the bad guy as far as my sister was concerned.'

'No. Even when she made a pass at me, I kept it to myself,' Alissandru bit out with suppressed savagery.

Isla shot him an incredulous look. 'You're not serious?'

'Che diavolo!' Alissandru exclaimed wrathfully, swinging away from her in an angry movement that revealed that that admission had slipped out of him in temper. 'It's true that it happened but it's not something I intended to tell you about. But if you think about it, it makes perfect sense. I was rich and very much the twin Tania would have preferred to marry and until she got to know me better she saw herself as irresistible.'

Isla swallowed hard, wincing for her sister at his admission, wishing he hadn't told her that salient fact, but she could remember Tania telling her that if she put her mind to it she could get *any* man she wanted. And Alissandru would have overshadowed Paulu to such a degree that Tania had eventually succumbed to temptation, Isla gathered unhappily. Alissandru might have been Tania's brother-in-law but he was also as flawlessly beautiful as a black-haired warrior angel in a stained-glass window. Even more gilded by his great wealth, her sister had unwisely decided to make a play for him.

'Drop the subject,' Alissandru urged curtly. 'It is a distasteful one. I am sorry I spoke so freely.'

Yet in a strange way, Isla was not sorry, for she felt as though she had finally learned exactly what lay behind Alissandru's loathing for her sister and her sister's loathing for him. Alissandru would never have forgiven such disloyalty to his twin while Tania would never have forgiven or forgotten such a rejection.

'You made me into the bad guy when you lost the baby,' Alissandru breathed in a fierce undertone. 'You closed me out, ran away—'

'I did *not* run away!' Isla launched back at him in furious rebuttal. 'I just needed a change of scene. And I didn't close you out, either…you were already on the outside!'

'Because I was too honest and I admitted that I wasn't sure the child you had conceived was mine?' Alissandru fired back at her. 'I didn't realise that you were a virgin. Blame that on the passion or my concussion…whatever you like. I didn't notice anything different. Blame me for the assumptions I made concerning birth control, too.'

'Oh, I already have,' Isla said tartly.

'But in the absence of proof of whose child it was, I assumed there was room for doubt and that you could even have been pregnant before you slept with me,' Alissandru intoned grimly. 'I'm a cynic. I won't apologise for the way my mind works but I am naturally suspicious when it comes to protecting my family or myself. I tend to assume the worst and act accordingly. But I was upset too when we lost our baby.'

Isla froze. 'Don't you dare tell me a lie like that!' she flared.

Alissandru swallowed hard. 'Regardless of what you think, for you to continue holding my innate caution against me even after I have done everything possible to be supportive is unjust.'

'Is it really?' Isla flung at him thinly as he lounged back against the ugly bar, effortlessly sleek and elegant in his designer suit, utterly untouched by the maelstrom of emotions that had tormented her for weeks. 'You ran as far and as fast as you could get from me in Scotland! You hated my sister! You accused me of sleeping with your brother! How do you expect me to feel about you?'

Alissandru breathed in deep and slow like a marathon runner readying himself for a race but Isla knew he was struggling to hang on to his temper. 'I didn't *run*,' he grated.

'You couldn't handle the fact that you had spent the night with Tania's sister! You assumed I was a gold-digging slut even though I was a virgin.'

'Your behaviour…the way you were dressed… at my brother's wedding led me to make certain ill-judged assumptions about the level of your innocence,' Alissandru bit out grudgingly.

An angry flush mantled Isla's cheeks. 'I didn't have much choice about what I wore that day. Tania told me she had a dress for me and I had to wear it because I had nothing else,' she admitted stiffly. 'It didn't fit and it was far too revealing but she said I had to wear it because it matched her silver wedding gown.'

That simple explanation irritated Alissandru more than it soothed because even he could not ignore the unreasonable bias that he had evidently formed against Tania's sister the very first time he'd laid eyes on her. He waited for her to say something about her behaviour that same day, something that would explain what she had been doing in a bedroom with his cousin Fantino, but when she said nothing more, his lean, strong face hardened. He had misjudged her but she was no angel and why should she be? A woman who could make him want her even when she was clad in furry fabric was obviously more of a temptress than even he had been prepared to acknowledge.

'Time for you to go,' Isla told him feelingly, colliding momentarily with smouldering dark golden eyes that left her short of breath and almost dizzy.

He was making her remember that night in Scotland and she couldn't stand that. The feel of his mouth on hers had created a chemical explosion that raced through her entire body, the magic sensuality of his hands had utterly seduced her. She had realised instantly why she had never been tempted into bed by any other man. Nobody had ever made her feel as he had.

'I'm not leaving until we have something settled about the house,' Alissandru intoned stubbornly.

Isla cocked a delicate coppery brow. *'Seriously?'* she jibed. 'You storm in here at nine o'clock on a Friday evening, force me out of the bath and demand that we do a deal about a house that I'm not even sure I want to sell yet? Do you think that's reasonable?'

Alissandru angled his arrogant dark head back, his lean, powerful body acquiring a stunningly insolent air of relaxation. 'I'm not in a reasonable frame of mind. I'm never in a reasonable frame of mind around you,' he murmured thickly.

'And why is that?' Isla prompted dry-mouthed, her skin prickling with sudden awareness, wicked heat darting up between her thighs.

His eyes, framed by slumberous black lashes, glinted like liquid gold. 'Because every time I see you I want you and that's all I can think about.'

'You did not just say that,' Isla whispered shakily, her face burning.

'Tell the truth and shame the devil,' Alissandru challenged huskily. 'All I want to do right now is rip that robe off you and sink into you over and over again...'

Isla trembled like a leaf in a high wind, fearful of being torn loose. *'Stop it!'* she told him fiercely.

'No,' Alissandru countered softly. 'When you came here, you knew this was going to happen. Deal with the consequences.'

Isla dealt him an aghast look. 'That is absolutely untrue.'

'You want me,' Alissandru traded without hesitation. 'You may not like it but you want me every bit as much as I want you.'

'You walked away!' Isla reminded him furiously.

'I had to force myself to do it and it didn't work. You've spoiled me for other women,' Alissandru husked, shameless eyes ranging over her with a stormy sexual promise that she felt bite to the very marrow of her bones. That look made her shiver. He emanated a shocking mixture of bold challenge and assurance.

She watched like a hypnotist's victim as he uncoiled his lean, rangy body from his lounging stance and moved forward. She couldn't breathe for excitement, couldn't move for fear of breaking his dangerous spell. He reached for her, all potent male and confidence, and he lifted her right up into his arms.

'We'll talk about the house tomorrow,' he told her. 'Once this is out of the way, we'll stop fighting.'

Was that true? she wondered weakly as he carried her up the stairs with the same ease with which he might have carried a doll. One more time, she reasoned wildly, clutching at his conviction that it would free them both from temptation.

'We mustn't… We *shouldn't*!' she protested more frantically as he identified the room she was utilising and strode through the door.

'We're not hurting anyone,' Alissandru grated with finality.

And it was true, she realised. As far as she knew nobody could be hurt by them being together. In any case, who would even know? As her brain careened madly from stop to go and then back to almost panic-stricken indecision, Alissandru kissed her with searing heat, forcing her lips apart for the scorching possession of his tongue. Something clenched hard deep down inside her and she started to tremble again, her head falling back, her lips parting, and the impatient drum beat of arousal pounded through her slender body like a storm she knew she had to quench.

CHAPTER SEVEN

WHY AM I doing this? Isla asked herself as she looked up at Alissandru in the dim light filtering up from the hallway. And it was so simple she could've screamed at the answer when it slotted neatly into place inside her head. She *wanted* him, just the way he had said she did; she couldn't control the craving, couldn't drive it out of her treacherous body, either. That craving was there, simply there, and it rewrote in an instant everything she had ever thought she knew about herself.

He yanked loose the sash on the robe, spreading it open slowly as he leant over her, unwrapping her with a care that suggested she was a very precious parcel. She didn't cringe the way she had at the croft, didn't try to hide herself, either. Instead, she listened to the catch in his breath and watched his face as he looked at her breasts with fierce appreciation. His hands lifted to cup the full swells, his thumbs rubbing at the swollen pink peaks as he stole another kiss, and her hands plunged into his luxuriant hair, fingers filtering through the silky strands and then dropping to his shoulders, unsuccessfully trying to come between them to pull at his jacket.

'I know… I know,' Alissandru ground out in similar frustration, backing away to unceremoniously yank the jacket off and tug at his tie with thrilling impatience.

Isla lay there, all of a quiver with heat and desire, just watching him undress. They had made love in virtual darkness at the croft and this time she was hungry for the details and curious. He tossed condoms on the bedside table and their eyes met, his defensive, hers troubled and evasive, and he came down beside her and kissed her again then as if his whole life depended on it. Breathless, Isla squirmed at the sleek, hot, heavy weight of him and then she arched as his mouth closed over a swollen nipple, drawing on the sensitised tip until she felt as though fire raced between her breast and her pelvis, stoking the slow burn of need rising between her legs. It was an ache, a sweet, hollow ache she couldn't bear.

'Touch me,' Alissandru said urgently, carrying her hand down over his hard, flat stomach.

And for a split second she froze, unsure of herself, afraid to do it wrong, and then she connected with the hunger in his intent gaze and she jerked as if he had lit a touchpaper inside her because it was the same hunger that drove her. Her hand stroked down the length and breadth of him. He felt like satin wrapped round steel but was infinitely more responsive, arching hungrily up to her touch.

Isla pressed him flat and lowered her head, closing her lips round him as she stroked, listening with helpless feminine amusement and satisfaction to the hoarse sounds and the ragged Italian words she dragged from him. A little more and he was dragging her up to him again, driving her lips apart with the hunger of his, twining his tongue with hers and delving deeper until she writhed against him, glancing into quite deliberate friction with the hard length of him.

'I intended to go slow but I can't wait. *Madre di Dio, bella mia*...what are you doing to me?' Alissandru groaned, sliding teasingly against the tender flesh at her core.

Without even thinking about what she was doing, Isla tilted up her hips to receive him, and he began to slide home with a sinuous circling of his lean hips and then he froze and yanked himself back from her again to reach for the condoms by the bed.

'What is it about you?' he exclaimed in raw disbelief. 'I almost forgot again and I swear *never* to make that mistake again!'

For a split second, Isla froze. *That mistake…* Their baby. Of course that was how he thought about that episode, and how could she blame him? An unplanned pregnancy with a woman he'd only intended to spend one night with? A big drama and a source of stress he could naturally have done without and he would be as keen as she to ensure that that oversight was not repeated. She could not understand why that sensible fact should make her feel so unbearably sad.

'I'm so sorry,' Alissandru grated as he came back to her and captured her reddened mouth hungrily with his. 'It won't happen again.'

That sensual assault unfroze her and mercifully threw her back out of her unhappy thoughts. She could think of nothing but Alissandru as he drove into her with potent energy and an unashamed groan of satisfaction, thrusting home to the very heart of her and sending such a jolt of stark pleasure through her that she cried out, her face warming in the aftermath. Sensation gathered with his every slick invasion, the tightening bands of muscle in her pelvis increasing the waves of excitement gripping her.

'Don't stop…oh, please, don't stop!' she gasped at the height of a spasm of pure bliss when her very existence seemed to depend on his next virile lunge and her heart was thumping so hard and fast she was breathless.

She hit the heights even faster in an explosive climax that threatened to jolt the very bones from her body, so all-encompassing was the experience. Sweet paroxysms of exquisite pleasure eddied out from her exhausted body and cocooned her in melting relaxation.

Alissandru cradled her in his arms, shell-shocked in the aftermath. Just as in their very first encounter, sex with Isla was sublime but he wasn't going to think about that, wasn't going to question anything, *anything at all*, he instructed himself grimly. A kind of peace, a peace that had evaded him for long torturous weeks, enclosed him.

'I didn't even ask you if it was okay…us making love again.' Alissandru registered that omission in dismay.

Isla sighed. It was fine, nothing left to worry about.

He awoke in the early hours and for an instant could not even work out where he was, and then he looked down at Isla and began to slide out of the bed, making a real effort not to disturb her. If he woke her, she would fight with him about something and then everything would go to hell again, he thought grimly. No, he would be discreet and tactful, even if neither trait came naturally to him, but he was getting better, wasn't he? He hadn't even mentioned being bitten by the rabid midget dog, had he? He would return home before he was missed and he would send Isla flowers and possibly something sparkly, because she didn't seem to own any jewellery beyond a watch and he wanted her to know how very much he appreciated being forgiven for his past excesses and awarded a second chance.

Isla woke up in a cocoon of contentment and then turned over and found Alissandru gone. She jumped straight out of bed, checked the bathroom and downstairs and realised with an angry stab of disbelief that he had walked out on her *again*…as if she was nothing, as if she was nobody, a one-night stand he could dismiss as soon as dawn folded in!

It was a painful moment of truth for Isla.

Alissandru had used her for sex. But hadn't she used him, too? She freshened up in the shower, her body tender and sensitised beneath her fingertips, and she thought of how he had woken her somewhere in the darkness of the night and made love to her again slowly and silently, but still with that dangerous, exhilarating edge of wildness that seemed to drive his passionate nature. Afterwards he had held her close, and she had felt sleepily, unquestioningly happy and secure.

Why did he have that effect on her when he had already done more to damage her self-esteem and hurt her than any man alive? Did her brain switch off when he was around? Did she have so little pride?

In the light of day, coming to terms with what had happened between them challenged her. She had wanted him and he had wanted her and it had seemed gloriously, wonderfully simple the night before. They weren't hurting anyone else, he had pointed out, but what about how *she* was being hurt? Losing their baby had already hurt her more than enough for one lifetime. Sleeping with Alissandru again would complicate their relationship even more.

Why wasn't she dealing with the reality that she had developed more feelings for Alissandru than was safe in such a scenario? He only wanted sex. Maybe that volatile temper of his spurred his lust for her but lust didn't amount to much, did it? It wasn't feelings, it wasn't caring…

Was that what she was looking for and had hoped to find with him? When she was at the point of tearing her hair out by the roots with frustration over her distinctly confusing reactions to Alissandru, Constantia arrived at the front door with Puggle.

Isla was as wreathed in blushes as a shamefaced teenager at being confronted by Alissandru's mother the morning after the night before. She invited the older woman in for coffee, apologised profusely for the messy kitchen and grabbed a tray to carry the cups out to the pretty terrace that overlooked a rather overgrown garden at the back of the house. Once there she concentrated on practicalities and asked if there were any local charities who might welcome a donation of clothes and things. Constantia was very helpful, and she asked Isla about her friendship with Paulu, visibly relaxing over the freedom to talk about her late son.

'Your sister made my son very, very happy,' the older woman said quietly. 'At times she also made him very unhappy but I am grateful for the happiness he did find with her.'

'Did you get to know Tania well?' Isla asked curiously.

'No. I was her mother-in-law and she was wary of me, fearful that I might be the interfering type. I've never been in this house before,' Alissandru's mother confided, startling Isla. 'Your sist⸺ never have invited me in. She gua⸺ ⸺acy fiercely.'

'I didn't get to know her well at all because she wasn't the confiding type and I can hardly blame her for that when I was so much younger,' Isla conceded ruefully.

'She was very independent, possibly because she was making her own living from an early age,' Constantia remarked reflectively. 'Alissandru and Tania clashed from day one but that was inevitable with them both being such strong-willed individuals.'

'I clash with Alissandru, too,' Isla heard herself confess and then was stunned that she had spoken so freely.

'That won't do him any harm.' Constantia's smile was warm with amusement. 'Alissandru always thinks he knows best. He was the same in the nursery...bossy and bold.'

'And quick-tempered?' Isla prompted helplessly.

'Oh, yes,' Constantia agreed. 'But the flipside of that was that he was also very honest and responsible. Paulu would've lied sooner than admit he had done something wrong but Alissandru was always fearless.'

When the bell went, Isla was mulling over that conversation while she guiltily cleaned the kitchen she had ignored the night before, but only because of Alissandru's unexpected arrival, she reminded herself wryly.

She went to the door and received an exuberant arrangement of white flowers, all ready for display in a sparkling crystal vase. She didn't need to read the card in the foliage but she opened it with compressed lips, scrutinising Alissandru's initials with reluctant amusement. He was being *very* discreet because there was no message or proper signature to reveal the identity of the sender.

When the bell went a second time, she was filling bin bags with Paulu's and Tania's clothing while
carefully checking pockets or bags for anything
that should be retained. This time it was a man in
a chauffeur-driven car who formally presented her
with a gift-wrapped shallow box, clicked his heels
with military precision and climbed back into the car.
Once again she found an initialled gift tag and she
rolled her eyes, ripping open the package with little
ceremony as she stood in the kitchen, which was
flooded with sunlight. A disconcerted look on her
face, she flipped open the shallow jewellery case and
the blinding sparkle of the diamond necklace within
knocked her for six. She lifted it out, stunned by the
shimmering rainbow glitter of the row of diamonds,
and rage engulfed her in a flood.

Alissandru thought he could give her diamonds
after spending the night with her? Some sort of pay-
off—a don't-ring-me-I'll-ring-you cop-out on decent
behaviour? Well, he could take a flying jump off the
edge of the planet!

She leapt into the hire car, Puggle accompanying
her, and drove up to the *palazzo*, powered on the fuel
of fury alone. The manservant, Octavio, whom Constantia had confessed ran her son's household with
the efficiency of the former soldier he had been, ushered her in and, when she requested Alissandru, es-

corted her at a stately pace along a corridor where he knocked on a door for her and then departed.

'Avanti!' Alissandru called.

Isla plunged over the threshold with the eagerness of a cavalry charge, stopping dead one foot in the door to press it closed behind her while glowering at Alissandru, who was seated behind a laptop at his desk.

'Isla!' he exclaimed as though she were a welcome, if unexpected, visitor.

He lunged upright, black hair untidy above startlingly bright dark golden eyes, a smile curving his sculpted mouth. He wore faded jeans and an open black shirt and was visibly in weekend relaxed mode. 'To what do I owe the honour?' he asked, feasting his attention on the vision she made in a rather shapeless grey linen shift, which should in his opinion have looked dowdy but which inexplicably merely set off her wonderfully vibrant hair and eyes and accentuated the grace of her slender limbs.

Unfortunately his dark deep voice, which was utterly seductive in the darkness of the night hours, acted on Isla like a flame thrower. 'Thank you for the flowers,' she told him curtly. 'But no thank you for the jewels!'

As she slapped the jewel case loudly back on his desk, Alissandru stiffened and frowned at her, dark brows pleating, stunning eyes narrowing beneath his curling fringe of black lashes. '*Cosa c'è che non va?* What's wrong?' he demanded, taken aback by her mood.

'If you spend the night with me, you don't pay for it with diamonds!' Isla informed him with fierce pride.

'It wasn't a payment, it was a *gift*,' Alissandru contradicted with emphasis, studying her with frowning intensity, wondering how something so simple could be interpreted as something so wrong.

'I don't want gifts *that* expensive!' Isla fired back at him. 'I won't accept them.'

'Duly noted,' Alissandru said drily. 'But does a poor choice of gift really demand this vehement a refusal?'

Isla bridled, reluctant to go into what had made her so very angry, determined not to betray herself in such a way. 'You offended me.'

'Obviously,' Alissandru conceded, marvelling that he had once believed she was a carbon copy of her infinitely more avaricious sister. 'But it was a gift, a small sign of my appreciation for the night we shared.'

Isla gritted her teeth. 'Staying around for breakfast would have been better received.'

'But that would have been indiscreet and I did

promise you discretion,' he reminded her silkily. 'If I'm home before dawn, nobody notices, but a later return attracts witnesses and I wasn't sure that you would be comfortable with a more public unveiling of our intimacy.'

Hot colour washed Isla's face in a slow, burning and very uncomfortable flush, because she didn't want anyone on the Rossetti estate knowing about that 'intimacy'. 'I want last night to remain a secret,' she told him without hesitation.

'Not a problem,' Alissandru agreed carelessly, stooping down to snatch up the document case that Puggle had dug his teeth into, contriving to lift both document case and dog together into the air.

Moving forward, Isla hurriedly detached Puggle and gave him a sharp word of reproof when he growled at Alissandru. 'Give him some food and he'll stop trying to bite you.'

'What about discipline? Training?' Alissandru suggested in wonderment. 'Wouldn't that be more sensible?'

'Food is quicker and easier, but if I don't watch out he's going to get fat.' Isla sighed.

Alissandru broke up a scone lying on the untouched tray to one side of his desk and dropped a chunk of it in front of Puggle. The little dog pounced on it with glee. There was good reason for Alissandru's generosity. He didn't fancy having to evade Puggle's sneak attacks at night in Isla's house.

'Coffee?' he proffered in the awkward little silence that had fallen.

'No, not right now. I'm busy clearing the house and, since it's not something I really want to be doing, I'd sooner get it done and finished,' Isla admitted in a rush, turning away in an uncoordinated circle, wanting to escape, wondering how he had managed to turn the situation on its head so that she felt as though *she* were the unreasonable one. 'I wondered what to do about Paulu's desk and personal effects.'

'If there's nothing you want I'll send someone over to collect them and bring them back here,' Alissandru said gravely. 'His desk is probably stuffed with estate paperwork and I should have that passed over to the new manager in case there's anything of interest.'

'Of course. Well, that's something sorted.' Isla wandered over to the window, which overlooked the wooded hills to the back of the house. 'I'm planning to stay here for a few weeks.'

'There's no pressure on you to make a decision about what you're doing or how long you're staying,' Alissandru hastened to declare, recalling how haunted she had been in the aftermath of the miscarriage and wondering how much of that regret she was still carrying.

'This is sort of a holiday for me before I get back to the real world,' Isla admitted.

'And what does getting back to the real world entail?' Alissandru asked, watching her as the sunlight gilded her hair into a multicoloured bonfire of curls, the pale perfect profile, the intense wariness of her stance as if she was waiting for him to say or do something she found objectionable and use that as an excuse to escape.

He had never met a woman like Isla before and to some extent it unnerved him because she was an unknown quantity. A woman who threw diamonds back in his face, *insulted* by them, he thought, marvelling at that lack of materialism. A woman who challenged him, stood up to him, went her own way regardless, unpredictable and in some ways as volatile as he was. An explosive combination. He gritted his teeth as the silence lay, his question unanswered.

'I'll probably go back to studying,' she confided somewhat grudgingly, as if giving such personal information went beyond the bounds of their relationship.

'Studying what?' he pressed, genuinely curious.

'I'd have to pass another course first but afterwards—assuming I'm successful—I think I'd like to go to university to do a paramedics course. I want something interesting, *active*,' she admitted, turning finally to look at him, her head tilting back because he was so tall.

'It would be challenging but I think you're strong enough to do it.' Alissandru stood there, his dark head at an arrogant questioning angle, his stunning dark golden eyes welded to her with intensity and a literal flame of heat ran over her entire skin surface, warming her within and without and in places she didn't like to think about. Her reaction was so instant it was terrifying and, feeling suddenly vulnerable, she turned her head away again and headed for the door.

'Oh,' she muttered, pausing on the threshold to glance back at him. 'A little hint if you're not too proud to take it. Your mother's ready for another dog. She adores Puggle and I think she would love a new pet.'

And with that helpful little assurance she was gone like quicksilver. Alissandru frowned even as he got on the phone to organise an employee to pack up and collect the contents of his brother's study. Isla was thoughtful, kind and intuitive. A new puppy would indeed comfort his mother, whose need for company he had failed to fulfil. Constantia had seen his brother daily and missed him the most while Alissandru had always travelled the world on business. It was true that he was home a great deal more than he used to be, but his conscience twanged that it had taken an outsider to point out a possibility that he felt he should've thought of first.

On her return to the house, Isla made a trip to two local charity shops. She was thinking about Alissandru far more than she felt comfortable with and deeply regretting her loss of temper. She had overreacted; she *always* seemed to overreact to Alissandru. She had overlooked the reality that a diamond necklace might be a *huge* gift on her terms but that it was a much lesser thing to a man of his wealth. Even so, she thought ruefully, it was better to have returned such an expensive present and to keep the difference in their circumstances out of the equation before it threatened to muddy the water and he started thinking she was a gold-digger again. Or did he still secretly think that anyway? She rolled her eyes at her meandering ruminations. She had no idea what Alissandru *thought* because to a certain extent she had already taught him to watch what he said around her.

On her return, it was a relief to see the contents of Paulu's study being packed up and removed. From those personal effects, she chose only a framed photo of the couple together on a beach somewhere, their smiling faces a good memory she wanted to conserve as her own. That and a little gold locket that had once belonged to her mother and that silly stool were the only personal items that Isla wished to keep from the house.

With Paulu's former assistant helping, Alissandru tackled a job he had long avoided, feeling almost grateful for Isla's part in virtually forcing him into the task.

'This is…er, legal,' his brother's secretary told him, passing him a folded document, complete with a notary's seal.

Alissandru frowned down at the local notary's stamp, wondering why his brother had approached another solicitor instead of Marco, the family lawyer. He opened it up and was disconcerted to discover that the document was another will and, what was more, a will drawn up and duly witnessed more recently than the one the family lawyer had had.

And that later will *altered everything*, Alissandru realised in sheer consternation. Only weeks before his death his twin had changed his mind about how he would dispose of his worldly goods, clearly having had second thoughts about leaving his home to anyone outside the family. He had left everything, house and money as well, to Alissandru, and Alissandru almost groaned out loud. Why the hell had Paulu changed his mind?

Alissandru suspected that Isla's advice had helped

his brother to win his wife back and, in that first instance of reclaiming Tania, gratitude had persuaded his brother to leave his estate to his sister-in-law, should both he and his wife die first. And then perhaps Paulu, an innate worrier, had begun to think about the risk of leaving such a will in his wake and the effect it could have on Alissandru.

Alissandru gritted his perfect white teeth. It had been wrong to leave the house away from the family estate but to leave that money to Alissandru instead had been an unnecessary gesture. *He* didn't need the money, but Isla *did*.

And how was Alissandru supposed to act to redress a situation that now threatened to become a messy injustice?

He would keep quiet. He would put the new will in the safe rather than lodge it with Marco Morelli, who would kick up a ruckus and, as the family lawyer, inform Isla immediately of the new will's existence. But was suppressing the new will in such a way illegal? Alissandru breathed in deep and slow. He didn't wish to break the law and, surely, it was *his* duty as Paulu's twin to ensure that his brother's last wishes were respectfully carried out?

He would lodge the new will with Marco and tell him that he did not wish it acted upon. Assuredly, as the main legatee, he must have the right to make that decision. He wanted Isla to keep the money, he only wanted the house and he was quite happy to *buy* the house back from her.

But what if Isla decided not to sell? Or chose to sell to someone else? The new will would be his safeguard, Alissandru decided grimly, a weapon only to be utilised if he was left with no other choice.

CHAPTER EIGHT

'PLEASE JOIN US for dinner this evening,' Constantia argued, reading Isla's reluctant face with accuracy.

'It's a family do,' Isla pointed out as the older woman regarded her expectantly. 'And I'm not family.'

'Your sister was my son's wife and you will always be family,' Alissandru's mother assured her reproachfully.

'I don't really have anything suitable to wear. I'm sure you all dress up.'

'Only Grazia, Alissandru's friend, really dresses up, but then she *is* a fashion designer. A plain dress will be sufficient.'

'I'm afraid I didn't pack anything fancy.' Isla sighed, every muscle in her body tensing at the reference to Alissandru's 'friend' as she struggled to combat an overpowering urge to demand to know who Grazia was and what her relationship with Alissandru was. Secret relationships were all very well until such complications appeared, she conceded ruefully.

But liking Constantia as she did and reluctant to risk causing offence, Isla laid out her only suitable dress that evening and put it on. It was a typical little black dress that wouldn't have raised a thrill even in its fleeting glory days when she had bought it to wear at a work dinner. She went a little heavier on her make-up than she usually did, painstakingly using eye liner and more mascara than usual. Grazia? Who was Grazia? Fierce curiosity powering her, she drove up to the *palazzo* where a whole collection of cars was already parked.

Constantia made a point of introducing her to everyone and, truth to tell, although there was some very flashy jewellery on display, a lot of the women were wearing little black dresses although the majority were fancier than her own. Some of the faces were familiar from that long-ago wedding but mercifully there was no sign of Fantino the Perv, as she thought of Alissandru's cousin. Of Alissandru and his 'friend' there was as yet no sign, but then there was a burst of chatter at the foot of the huge reception room where they were gathered for drinks and Isla glanced towards the door to see their host make an entrance with a tall slender blonde garbed in a tangerine dress with giant raised shoulders and a plunging neckline. He liked blondes, she thought first, and then, he liked blondes who *clung* because his animated companion was hanging on to him so tightly it was as if she feared that he might make a break for freedom.

Isla's observations mushroomed the more she watched them. The minute anyone tried to get into conversation with Alissandru, Grazia intervened, occasionally stepping between him and someone else or hailing someone else across the room and tugging him in that direction. The blonde was very pointedly possessive. She talked constantly, demanding his attention, stroking his sleeve, at one point stopping dead to straighten his bow tie in a statement of familiarity that made Isla's teeth grit.

It was an uncomfortable show for Isla to be forced to watch when Alissandru had been in *her* bed with *her* the night before. Was she jealous? Overly possessive? she asked herself worriedly, disliking the shrewish tone of her thoughts. As for Alissandru, she could read him even better in the slight widening of his eyes when he saw her; he hadn't expected her to be present and he moved with his companion in every direction but Isla's, and by the time they all moved into dinner, Isla was angry at being ignored.

As they were passing through the big hall towards

the dining room, Alissandru addressed her. 'Isla…
my mother didn't tell me that you would be here.'

'It was kind of her to ask me,' Isla parried lightly,
meeting Grazia's assessing dark eyes as Alissandru
performed an introduction.

'So, you're Tania's little sister,' Grazia remarked.
'You don't look much like her.'

'No.' Accustomed to such comments when anyone
had met Tania first, Isla merely smiled and added,
'Your dress is a wonderful colour…'

And that was all that was required to encourage
Grazia to tell the tale of how she had found the material in a Moroccan silk market and imported it
to make signature pieces for her most recent fashion show. They separated to find their seats and Isla
was reasonably happy with the way the meeting had
passed off. She hadn't scratched Grazia's eyes out.
She hadn't slapped Alissandru across the face even
though she was naturally wondering if he was sleeping with the beautiful blonde, as well.

Of course, she was going to wonder *that* when
the woman was all over him like a rash, touching
him with a level of familiarity that went beyond the
usual definition of friendship. So, decidedly not just
a platonic bond on Grazia's side, Isla decided, recognising that she was learning stuff about herself
through Alissandru that she had never dreamt she

would learn. She *was* the jealous, possessive type, she acknowledged with guilty unease. In fact, she found it very hard to look anywhere else in the room.

His mother should've warned him that Isla would be attending, Alissandru reflected impatiently, reading in Isla's stiff smiles and set little face all that he didn't want to see. Now she was furious with him, now she would be trying to throw him out of bed, her every suspicion aroused. The child they had lost had created a deeper bond between them but that extra layer both united and divided them, he conceded grimly. He cursed Isla's desire for secrecy and questioned how the hell he had strayed into so potentially chaotic an affair. In truth, he didn't know how he had ended up back in bed with Isla or why he had spent most of the day thinking about doing it again and revelling afresh in the hot, sweet welcome of her curvy body. Suddenly he was off-the-charts obsessed with sex for the first time since his adolescence and it had blinded him to every other consideration.

Isla was ridiculously unlike his previous lovers. She didn't look like them, didn't act like them, didn't think like them and was highly unlikely to respect his boundaries. Even more pertinently, those boundaries were set in stone: he didn't get attached, he didn't like strings or drama or plans for a future that stretched more than a week ahead.

'She's very jealous, isn't she?' Grazia whispered in his ear. 'She doesn't look the type to make a public scene, though.'

'What the hell have you been playing at?' Alissandru demanded grimly.

'I couldn't resist testing her out once you said she was here,' Grazia admitted. 'A woman who tosses back diamonds could be worth her weight in gold to a man like you.'

'What do you mean by a man like me?' Alissandru practically snarled back, so irate was he that Grazia was pot-stirring merely to amuse herself.

Grazia gave him a huge affectionate smile. 'Well, to be honest you've had it very easy with women. You click your fingers and they swamp you in attention, you ditch them and they still act like you're their best friend in the hope that you'll come back. And here you are having to *try* to impress a woman for the first time ever and she still won't even walk down the street in daylight with you,' she proffered. 'I think it's *precious*.'

'I shouldn't have told you about her.'

'Yes, but you didn't tell me *everything*, did you?' Grazia said with a shrewd knowing look. 'I sense more of a back story than you're willing to share.'

'Mind your own business,' Alissandru advised her bluntly, thinking that that was one back story he would never share with anyone.

Isla stayed as long as was polite, cutting out after coffee and walking back out to her car with a sense of crashing relief that she had escaped the source of her discomfiture. Well, one lived and one learned, she reasoned with herself, and over the course of the evening Isla had learned that sex on its own wasn't enough for her. Alissandru was a womaniser and she couldn't say that she hadn't been warned, not only by Tania's gossip but also by his no-holds-barred rejection at the croft. Two people as different as she and Alissandru could only be a bad fit.

And that was *that*, she told herself as she removed her make-up and got ready for bed. She wasn't about to punish herself with regrets because it had undoubtedly been time she acquired some experience with men. And she had run through the entire range of emotions with Alissandru, from the heartbreaking loss of their child to the sheer joy she had discovered in his arms. He had been useful for that, at least, she thought ruefully. Useful for that but not for much else, she extended censoriously. A very off-putting example too, she ruminated, terrific for sex, useless in every other sphere.

The doorbell went. Isla stiffened and ignored it. It went again, shrill and sharp as if it was being jabbed by an angry hand, the noise provoking Puggle into staccato barks. Isla climbed into bed and reached for her book while wondering if she should've gone downstairs to speak to Alissandru. She just knew it was him ringing the bell. What on earth would she have said, though? Another argument would not improve matters, particularly when she would have to deal with him to sell the house. No, it was more sensible to move on and ignore him and that meant no more thinking about him, no more wondering, no more dreaming. It occurred to her that life was suddenly looking very dull indeed.

Alissandru, unhappily, had no experience of being ignored and it inflamed him. Isla blew hot and cold. He never knew what she would do next. If she wasn't shouting at him or blocking him on her phone, she was shutting him out, hugging the charmed circle of her privacy and all that made him want to do was invade it. A sensible man, however, would just go home again and leave her to stew, Alissandru reflected grimly. But Alissandru never turned his back on a challenge. He walked round to the side of the house and calculated his chances of climbing up onto the roof of the kitchen to make it into the bedroom where she had left the window open. *Go home*, logic advised, confront Isla, his volatile, stubborn nature urged. Yanking loose his bow tie to unbutton his collar, he cast his jacket over a shrub and tested a drainpipe for stability.

Isla heard a noise and looked up from her book. As she saw a hand come through the window to grasp at the sill she screamed so loud that she hurt her throat.

'*Per l'amor di Dio*...it is only I,' Alissandru drawled as he pushed the window wider and swung lithely through the gap, black hair tousled as he leant back on the ledge and stretched, long, lean black-trouser-clad legs extended.

In the blink of an eye, Isla transformed from terrified paralysis into raging-shrew mode. 'What the hell do you think you're doing? You frightened the life out of me!'

'You should've answered the doorbell,' Alissandru pointed out drily, studying her slumberously from beneath luxuriant black lashes.

'How the hell did you get up here?' Isla demanded, leaping out of the bed to peer out of the window into the darkness below. 'You climbed up? You stupid idiot! You could've been hurt!'

'But I wasn't,' Alissandru pointed out silkily, trapping her between his spread knees, big hands curving to her shapely hips. 'I don't like to boast but in my misspent youth I climbed Everest. And I'm very grateful to arrive and discover that you are not wearing anything furry...'

Isla froze, embarrassingly aware that, having taken her by surprise, Alissandru had caught her bare of make-up and wearing the shortie pyjamas she had packed for warmer nights in Sicily. Suddenly the fabric felt as though it were shrink-wrapped to her dampening skin, and she went red.

'Although you do have rather eccentric taste in lingerie,' Alissandru purred, his attention locked to the frog print on the pyjamas. 'I will buy you something much more to *my* taste.'

Isla brought her hands down abruptly to break the spell, not to mention his hold on her hips, and she scrambled back into bed to say with as much cool as she could project, 'No, you won't be buying me anything *or* lingering to outline your fantasies. You're going to leave now...and sensibly, by the front door.'

Alissandru shook his dark head as if she had posed a question and sighed, stretching to loosen his shoulders, the front of his shirt rippling with the flexing fluidity of his muscles. Isla removed her attention from him quickly.

'What do you want?' she demanded tartly.

Alissandru dealt her a wolfish smile. 'I think you pretty much know what I want by now.'

Isla bridled. 'No. We're done.'

'Not as far as I'm concerned.'

'I didn't ask *you* how you felt about it!' Isla flung back at him in frustration.

'Why are you always angry with me?' Alissandru asked, frowning at her. 'I was your first, so I can't imagine there's a long line of bad guys who let you down in the past.'

'One of you is quite enough. Where did you stash your dinner date while you came here?'

'Grazia has gone home, probably laughing all the way,' Alissandru confided with sardonic bite. 'We've known each other from childhood as neighbours and friends. She's the sister I never had but I made the mistake of telling her about you before she arrived tonight, so she decided to play a game.'

'You told her about *me*?' Isla interrupted sharply. '*What* did you tell her about me? And since we're on a subject that *I* had no intention of raising, why does a woman you say you regard as a sister paw you like you're a cuddly toy?'

'To see if she could get a rise out of you...and drop me in it,' Alissandru told her with derision. 'She has an odd sense of humour, always did have.'

'What did you tell her about me?' Isla demanded accusingly.

'*Dio mio*... I didn't tell her anything too private...

believe me,' Alissandru countered grimly. 'There are some stories you don't share and *that* tragedy is one of them.'

The worst of Isla's tension drained away and her eyes softened, acknowledging that that wounding memory was theirs alone.

'She was overdoing the flirtation so much that you should've realised that it was fake. Do you really think I would be with a woman who behaves like that with me in public?'

'I don't know. I haven't seen you in public with a woman before,' Isla pointed out woodenly, feeling foolish, feeling mortified by the explanation he was giving her and not really knowing whether to believe him or not. 'Oh, go home, Alissandru. I've had enough of you for one night.'

'But I haven't had enough of you,' Alissandru murmured huskily, beautiful eyes of pure mesmeric gold holding hers.

Perspiration broke out all over her and she swallowed hard, fighting the flush of heat uncoiling at her core with all her might.

'And tonight was a game changer,' Alissandru intoned rawly. 'If you and I were out in the open, I would've been with you tonight, *not* Grazia, so from now on—'

'*No!*' Isla cut in forcefully, second-guessing what

he was about to say, her entire body freezing at the concept of their intimacy becoming public knowledge.

Everyone would know, she thought in horror. Everyone would think she was a slut to be sleeping with Alissandru five minutes after she arrived in Sicily and everyone would be a witness to her humiliation when it fell apart again. And what if somehow the story of the child they had lost came out? She turned cold to the bone at that fear because that memory was so very private. Her face suffused with angry colour because she knew what Alissandru was like, *knew* he didn't last longer than a couple of weeks with any woman, knew it would be foolish to imagine he would even last *that* long with her, a former waitress with no claim to fame or extraordinary beauty.

'Why not?' Alissandru asked silkily.

'I don't want people knowing,' Isla admitted without apology.

'Are you ashamed of me?' Alissandru studied her in angry fascination because he was used to women who wanted to show him off like a trophy.

Isla reddened. 'Of course not,' she muttered unconvincingly, still at war with her upbringing and the tenets that insisted sex was only really acceptable in a loving relationship. So, what did that make her? If she gave herself recklessly purely for pleasure? If she set her value so low she asked for nothing more? If other people saw those truths she would be humiliated, whereas what went on in private was strictly and literally her own affair.

'Either it's in the open or we're done here,' Alissandru delivered, rising fluidly upright, dark eyes glittering like golden blades.

Isla swallowed hard, unprepared for that direct challenge. It was an ultimatum as only Alissandru could make it. 'If we're out in the open where does that take us?' she prompted, playing for time.

'It may not take us anywhere,' Alissandru said bluntly. 'But at least it would be normal and I could share Sicily with you while you're here.'

'I'll think about it,' Isla muttered, plucking at the duvet with restive fingertips.

'Think harder, think now,' Alissandru instructed impatiently.

While you're here. A telling little comment. He didn't foresee them lasting for any appreciable length of time. But then, neither did she, so that was hardly a revelation. What did she have to lose? What did she most fear? *Losing him.* That revelation shocked her but it didn't change anything because either she chose to lose him now by choice or she faced losing him when she didn't want to in the near future. Did the baby she had lost make the idea of losing

Alissandru more threatening? Was that why she felt so bonded to him? She liked that explanation. But wasn't it time she took a risk in life? Let up on the need to protect herself and broke the rules of her grandparents, who had grown up in a very different era?

'All right,' she pronounced tautly.

Alissandru shot her a wicked smile and dug out his phone, pressing a number and shooting a stream of liquid Italian into it. He tossed it aside and began to unbutton his shirt, a long riveting slice of bronzed muscular chest appearing. 'From now on, you'll let me buy you things.'

Isla cocked her bright head to one side, dark blue eyes gleaming in her flushed face. 'Alissandru? Quit while you're ahead,' she advised. 'You're supposed to be generous in victory.'

Alissandru leant down and hungrily ravished her soft pink mouth with his own, his tongue delving deep. 'No, that's when I move in for the kill, *bella mia*.'

He shed his clothes without taking his stunning eyes from her once and it made her feel as if she was the only woman on earth for him at that moment. One moment in time, she told herself, one moment to feel *that* special, was worth whatever the aftermath would cost her. This time she watched him strip without turning her gaze away in uneasy denial of her curiosity. And there he was, glorious as a Greek god, completely male, all hard contours of bone and sinew, sleek bronze skin beautifully encasing lean, powerful muscles. The prominence of his arousal made her mouth go dry and she no longer marvelled at the soreness that had taken days to ebb after their first night together.

He ripped off the frog-print pyjamas without ceremony and flung them across the room, studying her pale curves with immense appreciation, lowering his head to stroke a swollen pink nipple with his tongue. Her breath caught in her throat and she recognised the surge of slick heat at her core, her hips shifting, her body primed and ready.

'Who were you phoning?' she asked shakily.

'I was ordering breakfast for us here,' Alissandru told her, long fingers tracing the scattering of freckles across the slope of her breasts. 'I'm not sneaking out like a cat burglar before dawn in the morning.'

'*And* you'll be using the front door from now on,' she muttered breathlessly.

'As long as you answer the bell,' Alissandru qualified.

Isla sent him a glimmering smile of one-upmanship. 'Then you make sure you treat me well,' she murmured, running a possessive hand down over his flat stomach, finding him, watching him react, his lush black lashes sinking low over his vibrant eyes.

'I think I can promise that,' Alissandru husked, turning over to find the centre of her and establish his ownership with a sure expertise that made her writhe.

She found his mouth again for herself, arching up to him, needy in a way she had never allowed herself to be before, her entire body screaming for her to rush to the finishing line.

Alissandru loosed a hungry growl as she pushed against him, startled to register that he was struggling to hold on to his control because Isla's need for him set him on fire. It had never been like that for him. He was as disciplined with sex as he was with everything else in his life, but his desire for Isla was hard to quench. He flipped her over onto her knees and sank into her with a hoarse sigh of unapologetic pleasure.

Isla was so excited she didn't know which part of her was more inflamed. Her heart was thumping so crazily fast it was threatening to burst out of her chest. She was on a sensitised high of receptiveness. The throb at the tender heart of her was almost unbearable and then he was there where she most needed him to be and the intensity of that first forceful plunge sent her flying higher than the stars, her body clenching tight and exploding with scorching sensation, leaving her clutching at the metal headboard of the bed to stay in position.

But the sweltering heatwave of pulsating response only continued as he increased his tempo, grinding into her with an insistent power that drove her straight onto another high. The fierce paroxysms of pleasure blew her away until she finally collapsed under him, catching his cry of release as he hauled her to him in the aftermath, melding their hot, sweat-dampened bodies together with an intimacy that she found incredibly soothing.

'It's never been like this for me,' Alissandru breathed raggedly, burying his nose in the soft springiness of her strawberry-scented curls, feeling the slight weight of her on top of him, shaken to experience the first glimmerings of renewed arousal at the same time. 'We light up the sky.'

'You walked away from it the first time,' Isla could not resist reminding him, because she took everything he said with a large spoonful of salt, determined not to overestimate her worth in his eyes.

'We barely knew each other,' Alissandru reminded her wryly. 'And maybe I did twin you with your sister more than I should've done...'

In the darkness, Isla smiled at that grudging concession, which she had thought she would never hear.

'But nothing lasts for ever...particularly at our

age,' Alissandru continued, to ensure that she didn't start thinking that their affair would be of the long-haul variety.

In silence, Isla gritted her teeth at that unnecessarily cool reminder. She didn't believe in fairy-tale happy ever afters. As a child she had continually dreamt that her mother would reclaim her and sweep her off to a more exciting life with her and Tania in London but it had never happened. In the same way as a teenager she had dreamt of the perfect man coming along and that hadn't happened, either. And then there had been the miscarriage and the loss of her first child. There had been few truly happy events in Isla's life and she was inured to disappointment. She preferred to concentrate on reaching more practical goals that would improve her life.

She would sell the house and get onto a course that would hopefully win her a place at university. As always work and effort would be what won her better prospects. With that thought in mind, she murmured drowsily, 'Relax, I'll be bored with you within a couple of weeks... You may be my "first" but you certainly won't be my last.'

The burn of hot liquid rage that flew up through Alissandru in answer to that forecast made him flinch. That was what he *wanted* to hear, he told himself decisively. It wasn't a rejection, or a criticism of his performance, it was only reality. In all likelihood he would get bored first, although he was anything but bored at that particular moment, he conceded grudgingly. There was no need to make a major production out of the discovery of great sex or imagine that it was anything more. No, the wiser approach was to make the most of any unexpected gift of pleasure and let the future take care of itself.

'I'm taking you shopping,' Alissandru announced at eight the following morning as he rifled through the wardrobe where she hung her few outfits. 'You haven't got enough clothes.'

'If you take me shopping you have to promise to keep your wallet closed,' Isla said quietly.

Alissandru ignored the proviso and tossed a plain white sundress on the bed. 'Come on, get up,' he urged impatiently. 'We're heading back to the *palazzo* for breakfast.'

'The *palazzo*? I thought you ordered breakfast to be delivered here?' Isla exclaimed in consternation, only halfway out of the bed. 'Besides, your mother's there.'

Alissandru groaned. 'My mother lives in her own entirely self-contained wing of the house and she would never dream of using the connecting door when I'm at home or I have a guest.'

Isla was unconvinced. 'But how will she know you have a…er…guest?'

'The staff will warn her.'

Isla sped into the bathroom, unnerved by the prospect of the staff that would report back to his mother, and then she scolded herself for worrying about something that was quite immaterial. Soon enough she would be leaving Sicily and only a vague memory because she was unlikely to ever return. What did it matter what anyone thought about her or her morals? Her grandparents had lived in a small tight-knit community where their reputation as a respectable family and the opinion of the neighbours had ruled their lives. Isla lived a much more anonymous life.

Alissandru noticed how Isla walked several steps away from him as if she were some chance-met stranger he had encountered on the drive and renewed irritation assailed him. He closed the gap and grabbed her hand to anchor her to his side, faint colour edging his cheekbones as she shot him a look of surprise. *Holding hands?* he derided. What the hell had he been thinking of? And how did he execute a smooth retreat?

Isla was disconcerted when Alissandru spun her close in full view of the *palazzo* and crushed her lips under his with all the enthusiasm of a man who had been held at bay for weeks. As he released her hand, she kissed him back, breathless and bubbling with sudden energy and happiness. She slid her hand shyly back into his before they headed for the front doors.

The dining room was a much smaller version of the room that had been used for entertaining the night before but, for all that, the table had been beautifully set with shining cutlery and beautiful crystal while Octavio was hovering beside a maid in charge of a large trolley.

'What do you usually eat for breakfast?' Isla asked casually.

'This morning I'm starving,' Alissandru confided with glinting amusement brightening his gaze as she coloured.

And Isla had to confess that, as soon as the silver domes were lifted on the cooked foods available, her stomach felt as though it were meeting her backbone.

Alissandru watched with satisfaction as Isla demonstrated the healthiest appetite he had ever seen in a woman and, having polished off a heaped plate, finished with a croissant and a cup of very rich hot chocolate.

'We have a busy day ahead of us,' he told her, lounging back in his chair.

'*We?*' she queried.

'It was your idea, so we're off to collect a puppy

on the other side of the island where the last pug came from,' Alissandru told her. 'I could have had the dog delivered but there's a litter and I thought you should choose, being a doggy kind of person, unlike me.'

Isla's attention briefly strayed to Puggle, who was fawning at Alissandru's feet in the hope of another titbit. 'Are you starting to like him?'

'I'm afraid not. He's a shameless manipulator and a crawler into the bargain,' Alissandru told her in disgust.

Isla laughed. 'He doesn't care what you think as long as you feed him. He's a dog, not a human.'

The sound of her amusement animated the formal high-ceilinged room, bringing a warmer, lighter element into the atmosphere. Alissandru frowned at her as though she were a riddle he had still to solve. He could not recall a woman ever making less effort to impress him. She didn't flirt or pout to hold his attention; she was happy to disagree with him and perfectly relaxed in his company. That resistance to being impressed made her an intriguing combination and a challenge. And although he was always exasperated by women who were clingy, he was keen to see Isla make more of an effort to attract him. Was that because no woman had ever made him work so hard for approval before?

He didn't know and he didn't much care. He was content to live in the moment. Isla wouldn't be in Sicily for long and he would make the most of their time together, keeping their affair light, casual and fun until it reached its natural conclusion.

CHAPTER NINE

'SO, YOUR FAMILY has always been rich and privileged,' Isla gathered without surprise, for Alissandru's awe-inspiring self-assurance was an integral part of his character. 'My background is very different. I come from a long line of poor people. My grandparents on both sides were crofters and they barely scratched a living. My father qualified as an engineer and he might have done better if an aneurysm hadn't killed him in his early thirties.'

'Why did your mother's parents raise you? Where was your mother?' Alissandru interrupted, reaching for the wine bottle to top up her glass.

'Trying to work two jobs down in London and take care of Tania at the same time. There was no way she could've coped with a baby, as well. She had poor health—she had kidney disease. There was never really any hope of the three of us reuniting as a family and living together,' she pointed out wryly,

covering her wine glass with her hand. 'No more for
me. In this heat too much would send me to sleep.'

'I believe I could keep you awake,' Alissandru
teased, dark golden eyes settling on her with slumberous sensuality, sending warm colour flying up
into her cheeks.

The remnants of a luxury picnic lunch spread in
front of them, they were sitting in a meadow that
gave them a bird's-eye view of the Rossetti estate. A
lush green collage of flowering orchards and vines
interspersed with the silvery foliage of the olive
groves stretched across the fertile rolling landscape
below them. That morning Alissandru had given
her a tour of the entire estate and, although Isla did
not feel she had been especially active, she was now
feeling ridiculously sleepy. Drenched in sunshine and
warmth, she stretched her shoulders, frowning as her
bra cut into her ribcage while, confined within the
tight bra cups, her tender breasts ached. Had she put
on weight? She supposed that was perfectly possible
when they had eaten out so often. Even when they
ate in at the *palazzo*, meals ran to several courses
and the food was rich.

But gaining a little weight wouldn't give her sore
boobs, she reasoned ruefully. She had thought that
was more likely to be linked to hormones and the
failure of her menstrual cycle to return to normal

and stay normal after her miscarriage. But how could she possibly consult a doctor here in Sicily about something so intimate when she didn't speak the language? In the same way she had baulked at asking Alissandru to organise birth control for her. All such matters could surely safely wait until she returned to London…although by then she would no longer have any need for birth control, she conceded with innate practicality.

Ought she be doing a pregnancy test? For goodness' sake, how could she be pregnant again? Apart from that one tiny moment her first night in Sicily with Alissandru, there had been no mishaps, no oversights. And yet sore breasts and absent periods were also the most common sign of pregnancy in a woman, she reminded herself worriedly, and there and then she decided that she would be perfectly capable of identifying a pregnancy-test kit in a Sicilian pharmacy. She would do a test simply to rule out that frightening possibility.

Alissandru rested back on one elbow watching her, wondering what she was thinking about that made her look so serious. He could barely credit that she had already been in Sicily for six weeks and that he had stayed with her that long, as hooked on the pleasure she gave him now as he had been at the outset. Six weeks had to be some kind of new re-

cord for him. But then Isla was intelligent and easy
company and he had enjoyed seeing Sicily through
her more innocent and less critical gaze. But when
would the boredom, the itch to move on to fresh
fields, kick in? He had also done the bare minimum
of work since her arrival, an acknowledgement that
disconcerted him.

Of course, that was what living in the moment en-
tailed, he reminded himself bracingly and, since he
hadn't taken a proper break in years from his work-
aholic schedule, it made sense to make the most of
his time with Isla because she would not be in Sicily much longer. She had already applied to join an
educational course in London, which started in the
autumn. He assumed that she was planning to stay
the summer, but he hadn't actually asked because he
didn't want to give her the wrong impression, and
looking that far ahead would definitely give her the
wrong impression.

Isla lay down, her drowsy gaze welded to Alissandru's flawless bronzed profile, experiencing that revealing little kick in her pelvis that made her squirm,
her body lighting up as if in search of him. That she
couldn't imagine life without him now terrified her.
Fleeting moments of happiness had always been the
norm for Isla, but the kind of effervescent happiness
that Alissandru gave her was an entirely new depar-

ture for her. She had not slept alone a single night since they got together and if business or travel intervened, Alissandru was not above joining her in bed in the middle of the night or even at dawn. Either she slept in his giant carved mahogany four-poster bed or he shared her far less ostentatious double at his late brother's house.

Recovering from being part of a couple and adapting to being alone again would be difficult for her. She had never imagined that togetherness developing when their affair began. She had assumed there would be days they wouldn't see each other, arguments when they rubbed each other up the wrong way and needed a break. But she had assumed wrong because she was with Alissandru round the clock and he didn't seem bored...*yet*. In addition, they had very few rows.

Dissension usually broke out when Alissandru tried to give her some ludicrously expensive gift and took offence at her refusal. He didn't seem to grasp that she didn't need presents to feel appreciated. She was much more impressed when he took the time to drive her up into some remote mountain village and walk her along narrow cobblestone streets to a tiny restaurant he had been told offered superlative but simple food, made of the finest, freshest ingredients. Or when he had taken her to see the Greek temple ruins in the beautiful valley at Agrigento even though he was not remotely interested in antiquity.

Yes, Alissandru was just chock-full of surprises, she conceded warmly. If he hadn't told her she would never have guessed that he had originally planned to be a doctor, but that he had abandoned his studies after his father's death because his parent had made some rather risky investments and the family finances had required a steady hand. That he had put his family's needs first had shown her how much caring he was capable of, and that he missed his twin every day was also a fact that touched her heart because, quite honestly, Alissandru had had very little in common with Paulu, yet he had still managed to love and value his brother.

'Just drop me at the house. I need to go to the pharmacy for…er…sun block,' she told Alissandru as she climbed back into his sports car.

'It's a five-minute drive into San Matteo. I'll take you,' Alissandru insisted.

And Isla thought about arguing and then worried that that would only draw attention to any purchase she made. Buying a pregnancy test was ridiculous, she told herself irritably. There was no way she could've fallen pregnant again. Even so, it was wise to rule out the possibility, however unlikely it was, she reasoned.

San Matteo was a pretty little town with a charming *piazza* surrounded by several cafés that overlooked the old church and the central fountain. Alissandru parked and said he would meet her at the bar next door to the pharmacy and she sped off. Recognising a pregnancy test on the shelf was not as much of a challenge as she had feared and she dug the package deep into her capacious bag and rejoined Alissandru with a smile on her face to enjoy a cold drink.

Driving past the *palazzo*, Alissandru glanced at the sleek car parked there and suddenly braked. 'Fantino and his mother must be here for lunch. Why don't you join us?'

Isla froze. 'Your cousin…er… Fantino?'

'*Sì*, you probably met them at my brother's wedding. I'm not particularly fond of Fantino but our mothers are sisters and close,' he explained wryly.

A chill ran over Isla's skin at the mere idea of even being in the same room as the man who had taken advantage of her youth and inexperience in a manner that had taken her months to recover from. 'No, thanks. I don't like Fantino.'

'You remember him?' Alissandru's voice emerged with an instinctive chill as he recalled what he had witnessed on the day of his brother's wedding. Reminding himself that Isla had been a mere teenager at the time, he just as quickly strove to forget the memory again.

'Yes, I remember him,' Isla responded woodenly. 'Just drop me back to the house...or I could walk from here if you like.'

His black brows drew together as he studied her pale, set face. 'What's wrong?' he prompted.

Isla breathed in slow and deep and then saw no reason to withhold the truth.

'Fantino assaulted me at the wedding.'

'Say that again,' Alissandru murmured more quietly.

'You heard me the first time,' Isla retorted curtly. 'I don't want to see Fantino or have anything to do with him.'

'That's a very serious allegation,' Alissandru pointed out harshly.

'Yes, and considering that he got away scot-free with what he did at the time, I don't feel any need to justify the way I feel now. Please take me home.'

Alissandru drove her back to the house in silence, his lean, darkly handsome features clenched with tension. 'We have to talk about this.'

Isla climbed out, her face still stiff. 'It's a little late in the day to talk about it.'

'And whose fault is that?' Alissandru shot at her, snapping the key for the front door from her nerveless fingers. 'If something happened between you at the wedding, we—my mother and I—as your hosts should've been made aware of it!'

Anger gusted through Isla in a heady wave as she stalked into the house, her vibrant curls bouncing on her shoulders, her dark blue eyes outraged. 'I made Tania aware of it and she said I wasn't to tell anyone else. Believe me, it happened! And it *wasn't* "between us", either. When a man assaults a woman, it *isn't* always a shared misunderstanding!'

'Tell me exactly what happened!' Alissandru urged her as she paced uneasily round the lounge.

'Tania sent me upstairs to her bedroom to fetch her bag and your cousin followed me. He tried to kiss me and he put his hand inside the neckline of my dress and tried to touch my breast!' Isla recounted with a helpless shudder of recollection. 'He said something disgusting and when I pushed him off me, he fell over the bed, which gave me the chance to get away. Of course, he was drunk and he thought it was all very funny and he started laughing. But I was scared and I was very upset. I was only sixteen, Alissandru… I'd never been touched before and I didn't know how to handle it.'

His eyes flared as golden as flames in his lean, strong face. The mere idea of Fantino touching sixteen-year-old Isla appalled Alissandru, most particularly because he had seen Isla leave that bedroom closely followed by his cousin and he had put entirely the wrong interpretation on what he had seen. The guilt of that shocking misconception hit him hard. He had caught a glimpse of a suspicious scenario and, instead of immediately being concerned about the welfare of a very young girl, he had assumed she had either been flirting or having sex and had done and said nothing. That awareness went right to the very heart of the prejudice she had accused him of harbouring, and in that instant he knew he could no longer deny that his low opinion of Tania had automatically encompassed her kid sister as well and had coloured his reading of the situation.

'I am so sorry that happened to you, but Fantino will be even sorrier!' Alissandru swore in a raw undertone, throwing back his broad shoulders. 'But I am also sorry that I did not intervene when I might have done that day.'

.'How could you have intervened?' Isla questioned without comprehension.

'I saw you coming out of that bedroom. I didn't see your face, just your back view, and then I saw Fantino coming out some seconds after you. I'm ashamed to admit that I simply assumed you had been having some sort of sexual or flirtatious encounter with him. I didn't question it.'

It was Isla's turn to stiffen and stare at him in shock. 'You thought that at sixteen I would go into a bedroom with a man and have sex in someone else's house? How could you think that of me at that age?'

'I have little justification but I *did* think that,' Alissandru admitted reluctantly. 'From the minute I saw you wearing the low-necked dress your sister put you in, I decided that you were just like her.'

Isla groaned, suddenly seeing the whole history of her relationship with Alissandru rewritten in the blink of an eye. He was finally acknowledging that that prejudice had existed, though, and that was a relief, she told herself soothingly.

'I am sickened that you suffered such an experience in my home. You should've been safe there. You were very young. In the absence of a parental figure, it was my duty to look out for your well-being…and obviously I failed,' he bit out grimly. 'On the other hand, Tania was very wrong to persuade you to keep quiet about the assault.'

'Alissandru… I didn't know any of you and I couldn't have brought myself to share that story with anyone I didn't know well. I felt humiliated and embarrassed. Tania suggested I might've encouraged him in some way while I was downstairs,' Isla told him. 'But I hadn't even spoken to him when he followed me up to that bedroom.'

'Do you want me to call the police? A sexual assault is a sexual assault, regardless of how much time has passed.'

Isla stiffened. 'No, I don't wish to make an official complaint. I've put it behind me now but I wouldn't want to meet him again or be forced to pretend that what happened didn't happen.'

Alissandru nodded gravely, his dark golden eyes glittering pale like shards of broken glass below his black lashes. He was thinking of the family jokes told about Fantino's persistent approaches to any attractive woman available. Maybe that wasn't quite so funny now that Alissandru was seeing the other side of the coin and having to question his cousin's behaviour. It had never crossed his mind to look on Fantino as a sex pest but that now seemed more accurate. That he should've dared to frighten and distress a young guest in Alissandru's home was inexcusable. He was also thinking guiltily that he too had noticed Isla's attraction that day and had dealt with it less than honestly by telling himself that she was a shameless little baggage. But he would never have acknowledged that attraction to so youthful a girl, *never* have given way to it.

'What the hell was Tania thinking of when she silenced you?' he ground out on his purposeful path back to the front door.

Wincing, Isla looked pensive and wry. 'That it would've wrecked her wedding…and it *would've* done. Imagine the atmosphere it would've created if I'd publicly accused Fantino! I was a complete stranger in a foreign country and Tania was almost as unknown to your family as I was at that stage,' she pointed out ruefully. 'Would anyone even have believed me?'

'Certainly, I hope we would have.' Alissandru breathed in deep. 'But it will be dealt with now as it should've been then.'

'Why… What are you going to do?' Isla asked worriedly.

'Deal with Fantino,' Alissandru bit out wrathfully. 'What else?'

'So, you believe me,' Isla gathered.

'Of course, I do.'

A moment later, he had gone and once the sound of his car had receded Isla paced the wooden floor, amazed at how shaken up she felt after getting that episode six years earlier off her chest. *Finally.* Her shoulders slumped and she felt relieved that that horrible secret was now out in the open. Naturally, she hadn't shared the story with her grandparents, who would've been horrified. But she had also kept quiet because she had feared that if they knew they would not let her travel alone again and back then she had still harboured the hope that the wedding invitation would lead to other invites from her sister. Of course, that hadn't happened and the sad repercussions of her encounter with Fantino had lasted a lot longer. For years she had been nervous of men, fearful of an assault coming her way without warning, fearful that something she might wear, say or do might attract such treatment. But she had moved past that eventually, survived, she reminded herself calmingly as she tripped over her bag, which she had abandoned in the hall.

Recalling the pregnancy test in her bag, she pulled it out. In the almost bare study, she lifted the dictionary of Italian words she had bought so that she could translate the directions. Fortunately, the pictorial diagrams were more easily understood and she decided to do the test immediately, rather than stress about it or be forced to attempt to do it when Alissandru was around.

He had been very much shocked by her story about Fantino, she acknowledged, but he would be a great deal more shocked, she reckoned, if she was to conceive again. It wasn't possible, she told herself as her heartbeat kicked up tempo. Her stupid hormones were still out of sync after the miscarriage and she would have to see a doctor when she got home again. Having convinced herself that the test was a simple formality to rule out an unlikely development, she went upstairs.

Fifteen minutes later, she was reeling in shock at what was undeniably a positive pregnancy test. Having returned her hire car some weeks before, she climbed into the little runaround that had once belonged to Tania and drove back to the pharmacy to buy a second test. Just to be on the safe side, she told herself. An hour later, she contemplated the second positive result and felt so dizzy and sick with nerves that she could barely breathe. After a few minutes she stood up and went to lie down on top of the bed and think.

Pregnant...*again*! How was she supposed to deal with the joy rising inside her and the quite opposite effect her news would have on Alissandru? How could it have happened when they had tried to be careful? Yet she knew that no contraception was foolproof. Her head swimming with confused feelings, she tried to imagine telling Alissandru *again* and immediately thought that maybe she *didn't* need to tell him this time, that maybe she should wait a few months to at least be sure she stayed pregnant.

She was, however, too sleepy to agonise for long and, while her conscience warred against keeping any secret from Alissandru, she couldn't help recalling the angst she had roused with her last announcement. Was she incredibly fertile? Was he? Would she manage to carry her baby to term this time around? Anxiety struck then and struck hard and she had to blank out her worries quite firmly before she could drift off to sleep, while telling herself that she would make decisions and worry about the consequences later.

The shrill noise of the doorbell woke her and, blinking sleepily, she scrambled up, stuffing her feet blindly back into the shoes she had kicked off while at the same time calling out to silence Puggle's frantic barks. She padded hurriedly downstairs and swung open the door on Alissandru, and that fast her cheeks burned and she ran an uneasy hand through her mussed curls.

'I have someone here who has something to say to you. It won't take long,' Alissandru murmured bracingly.

Isla spotted the car pulled up behind Alissandru's and stiffened in dismay as she spotted Fantino's weedy figure heading towards them. 'What does he want?' she hissed.

She didn't have to wait long to find out. Fantino had come to offer heartfelt apologies and regret for the distress he had caused at her sister's wedding and to insist that he would never do such a thing again. He made no excuses, offered no defence, merely concluding his awkward little speech with the assurance that he would be making a big effort to improve his behaviour. Isla studied the bruising and swelling on his thin face and swallowed hard, recognising that he had taken a beating and guessing by the granite-hard set of Alissandru's jaw that he had been the one to administer it. Jungle justice, she thought ruefully, but if it stopped Fantino in his tracks the next time he saw an attractive woman and made him think twice, she had no quarrel with the punishment.

She accepted the apology and watched Fantino jump back into his sports car with a curled lip.

'He will stay away from the estate while you're here,' Alissandru assured her.

'Did you have to beat him up?' Isla asked uncomfortably.

'I had to get the truth out of him…and I did,' Alissandru countered levelly, unable to explain even to his own satisfaction what had ignited the sheer rage that had gripped him once he'd got his hands on Fantino. The concept of anyone laying a single finger on Isla without her permission had incensed him. The awareness that she might not be his cousin's only victim had made him even angrier and determined to keep a watch on Fantino to ensure that he kept his promises to reform.

'I didn't want any violence, and your mother

must've been very upset by all this,' she muttered
ruefully.

'A generation back, a man could've been killed for
any action that could damage a woman's reputation.
Community disapproval controlled bad behaviour.
My mother is only upset that you did not feel you
could trust us with the story of what happened to you
that day,' Alissandru explained grittily. 'Now, if you
are in agreement, let us bury this matter.'

Isla nodded vigorously. 'Yes.'

'I have a fundraiser for a children's hospice that I
support to attend this evening,' Alissandru told her.
'Will you accompany me?'

'If it's black tie, I have nothing to wear.'

'Grazia has already offered to provide you with
a suitable dress,' Alissandru cut in. 'She'll be present tonight and would like to see you again. She is
probably planning to ask you at least a hundred nosy
questions.'

Isla looked up into his lean, darkly handsome face
and tried to face telling him what she knew she had
to tell him and she lost colour and dropped her head.
'Thank her for her offer. It's a very generous gesture, but I'm afraid I'd prefer to spend a quiet evening here.'

'You've had a distressing afternoon,' Alissandru
conceded reluctantly, studying her with his shrewd

gaze, picking up on her pallor and the shadows of strain below her eyes, wishing he could give her thoughts a more positive turn, wishing that Fantino's sleazy behaviour hadn't cast a pall over their day, for there was no denying that it had with Isla looking so drawn and fragile.

'A quiet evening and a good sleep will do me good,' Isla declared with a forced and brittle smile.

'How important is it that you sleep alone?' Alissandru asked bluntly, a long forefinger tracing the ripe curve of her lower lip. 'Because I don't sleep so well without you…'

Her dark blue eyes flew wide, her heart thumping at the smouldering appraisal he was giving her. It sent wicked little tingles coasting through her, started up a hot, needy throb at her core. *Because I don't sleep so well without you…* That was a statement that threw her heart wide open, filling her with dangerous warmth and an almost overpowering desire to throw herself into his arms. He was going out without her but he still wanted to spend the night with her.

Alissandru bent his dark head and kissed her, savouring the softness of her lips and the sweetness of her instant response, fierce arousal threatening his self-control and just as quickly unnerving him. You can go *one* night without her, he told himself irritably. You're *not* an addict. Why was everything with Isla so blasted complicated? He thought of Paulu's second will, which he had lodged with Marco, and suppressed a heavy sigh. He had felt foolish when Marco had erupted in approval of that discovery on the family's behalf when he knew he had no intention of having the contents of that second will actioned. Should he already have explained that decision to the family lawyer? But admitting that he was in a relationship with Isla had struck him as too private a revelation to make to one of his employees. If further explanation was required in the future, he would deal with it then, he thought in exasperation.

'I'll call you tomorrow,' he told her abruptly, releasing her to stride back to his car.

Isla stood there a few seconds longer, wondering what had happened, wondering why he had changed his mind about joining her after the fundraiser. She wandered back indoors, feeling strangely unsettled by her recollection of the sudden detachment that had momentarily frozen Alissandru's lean dark face, banishing his usual smile. Maybe he was getting tired of her, maybe he was only just beginning to realise that, she reasoned.

And how did that make her feel? As if the roof was about to fall in, she acknowledged guiltily, taken aback by the awful hollow sensation that filled her when she thought of Alissandru walking away from her. She had got attached, hadn't she? Seriously attached in spite of all the signs that he was not in the market for any kind of commitment. And even worse, now she was pregnant and that fact was more important than her feelings or his.

Isla walked around the house, busying herself with tidying up while she pondered her dilemma. There was really no avoiding the obvious. Alissandru had always been honest with her and she owed him the same honesty. A couple of hours later, her nerves nibbling at her in painful bites, she showered and changed and drove up to the *palazzo*, trying not to ask herself how it would feel when she saw angry resentment and regret in Alissandru's face when she told him she had once again conceived. As ever impervious to mood, Puggle danced at her heels, eager to see Constantia or Alissandru, both of whom could be depended on to feed him.

As she mounted the steps, a thickset older man emerged and hesitated. 'You must be Tania's sister, Isla,' he guessed as he extended his hand. 'I'm Marco Morelli, the Rossetti family lawyer.'

Isla tensed at the explanation. 'I suppose you'll be getting together some papers for me to sign,' she remarked, thinking of the legalities of selling the house back to Alissandru. She had already nominally agreed to sell the house back to him but the sticking point was that she was only willing to accept market value while Alissandru seemed to think that it was somehow his duty to pay very generously for it.

The older man frowned and shook his head in grave dismissal. 'No…there's nothing. A mistake that none of us could know *was* a mistake is already being rectified. Now that the new will has been lodged, it is merely a question of sorting out the tangle Paulu left behind him. I am sorry you have had this experience.'

Isla had fallen very still. '*New* will?' she queried breathlessly.

'Alissandru said that he would explain it all to you.' Marco Morelli checked his watch and sighed. 'Unfortunately, I have another call to make and I can't go into the complexities of a more recent will turning up and reversing the original right now, but if you have any questions, I would be happy to answer them for you at my office. Perhaps tomorrow… or the next day?' he prompted helpfully.

'So, there's nothing for me to sign,' Isla managed to gather, striving to act normally rather than betraying the reality that she had been dealt a body blow.

'No, once you return the inheritance the matter is fully concluded,' he assured her cheerfully. 'I know Alissandru wishes to compensate you for this most regrettable confusion but, to be frank, he owes you nothing because he was no more aware of the second will's existence than anyone else. I persuaded him that he had to have the will lodged legally with the courts if he wanted to avoid further complications.'

· The older man bid her good day and hurried back to his car, leaving Isla standing there like a stone statue.

Slowly, very slowly as if her very bones ached, she retraced her steps to Tania's car, Puggle lagging behind her. She knew she couldn't face Alissandru at that moment. She had to gather herself, work out what to do next…aside from repaying what she owed. It was as if her life were a deck of cards that someone had tYhrown up into the air and now everything had changed radically.

Her independence, her plans, everything she had depended on was being torn away. Just her bad luck, as the lawyer had said. From somewhere, Alissandru had obtained another will and, within it, Paulu had presumably left his worldly goods to his brother instead. Isla was shattered. She remembered the contents of Paulu's desk being taken away and surmised that that was most likely where the second will had been found. Even she knew that a more recently dated will would take precedence over an earlier one. But Alissandru had seemingly learned about that will *weeks* ago!

Yet he still hadn't told her. The house was already his yet he was even now determined to *buy* it from her. Why? Because he *pitied* her. Her self-esteem squirmed as though it had come into contact with something very nasty and hurtful. And she was hurt, seriously hurt that he had not told her about that second will as soon as he became aware of its existence.

Knowing that Alissandru had seen her sister as avaricious, she had made a big effort to keep Alissandru's wealth out of their relationship. Pride had demanded that she stand on her own feet and Paulu's legacy had made it possible for her to do that. But now that financial security had vanished. And, even worse, it left her broke and in debt to Alissandru because everything she had spent in recent months, after being given access to Paulu's money, had not been *her* money to spend. How was she ever going to repay that money?

Thank goodness she hadn't spent like a lottery winner, she thought heavily. Her native caution with money had meant that she was careful, but she had spent a fair bit of money simply travelling to Sicily and had been living off it ever since. How could he not have told her about the second will?

It had been a lie of omission. Feeling sorry for her, Alissandru had kept quiet. He had planned to virtually pay her off by paying for a house he already owned and he would never have told her the truth because he would've let her walk away with his brother's money. And now she was pregnant and she was going to cost Alissandru even *more* money. She would be the financial liability he had never wanted.

Hot tears of mortification burning the backs of her eyes, she entered the house that was no longer hers and went upstairs to pack. She would return to London. What else could she do? She had to find herself some way of making a living again, at least until the baby was born. But no way was she about to tell Alissandru about the baby now face-to-face, not with this horrible financial bombshell engulfing her at the same time. She felt devastated and humiliated and taking herself quietly away seemed like her only dignified option.

She would write Alissandru a letter. That way, he could curse and storm when he found out that there was to be another baby. He wouldn't be forced to be polite; he wouldn't be forced to hide his true feelings. Once the dust had settled on that revelation, she would get in touch with him again.

She went online to see how soon she could get a flight to London but ran into difficulties when it came to travelling with Puggle. Travelling with a dog across Europe could not be done without foresight and planning. Puggle had to receive an injection several days prior to travel and she would need to arrange that first. Constantia would take him, Isla thought ruefully, but when would she ever be able to return to Sicily to reclaim him? Furthermore, leaving her dog with Alissandru's mother would entail making explanations she had no desire to have to make.

Writing a letter to Alissandru took Isla hours. After several failed attempts, she decided to keep it simple. She admitted that she had found out about the second will and that she had no alternative other than to vacate the house. She made no promises of repayment because, with neither a home nor employment awaiting her in London when she finally got there, there was little point in talking about what she couldn't deliver. She wrote about the baby in bald terms and assured him that she would get in touch once she was settled again.

Hearts didn't really break, she told herself firmly as she walked out of the house with Puggle confined in his carrier. She would recover...*eventually*. Alissandru had not encouraged her to fall in love with him. He had been quite clear from the outset that they were simply having a casual affair. Now she needed to concentrate on finding a local veterinary surgeon and somewhere she could stay with a dog in tow.

CHAPTER TEN

ALISSANDRU DROVE HOME from the fundraiser and the whole way he assured himself that he was giving Isla a night of unbroken sleep. But his foot hovered over the brake as he reached the *palazzo* and failed to connect, ensuring he drove on in the direction of his twin's former home. Isla had had an upsetting day and it was natural that he would want to check on her to ensure that she was all right, he reasoned ruefully.

The house was in darkness, which he hadn't expected because it wasn't late. Anxious now, he banged on the door, wondering if she had fallen asleep, and, when even that failed to rouse her, he dug out the key he had always had but neglected to mention and stuck it in the door. He called out her name, switched on lights, frowned and took the stairs two at a time, striding into her bedroom to find it empty. Where was she? The dog was missing, as well.

Obviously she had gone out. Was she with his mother? Since his mother had got the puppy, she had been communicating regularly with Isla about dog training. As if Isla could tell anyone anything about dog training, Alissandru reflected wryly. He called his mother to ask if she had company and, while she was telling him that she had not, he finally noticed the letter lying on the bed with his name printed on it.

As he read the first paragraph, which mentioned her unexpected meeting with Marco, he froze and he cursed. When she referred to her having left, he wrenched open the wardrobe door so roughly it almost fell off its hinges. It was empty. *Per l'amor di Dio...* Isla had *left* him. Alissandru was stunned into momentary paralysis. He hovered in the centre of the room and tried to entertain the concept of Isla being gone. No, he wasn't addicted to her, maybe a little obsessed...occasionally. Isla *gone*.

The shock of that knowledge made him sit down on the side of the bed because his legs turned weirdly weak. He returned to the letter with renewed interest and then reached the section about the baby on the way again and suddenly, in the midst of his turmoil, Alissandru was smiling. What was it about them? They got together and five minutes later...hey, no complaints, Alissandru reflected abstractedly, enthusiasm at the prospect leaping through him. Isla was going to have *his* baby. Obviously they were meant to be. It wouldn't have happened again, he reasoned, if the fates hadn't intended it so.

Alissandru smiled, temporarily in a world of his own, and then he unfroze. Isla had walked out on him when she *needed* him. He couldn't live with that awareness. In fact, it filled him with panic. Where was she? How was he to track her down? Could she have flown out of Sicily already? Should he go to the airport first?

His mobile buzzed, and he snatched it up.

It was Grazia and he only answered it because, if he didn't, Grazia would simply keep on ringing and ringing.

'Alissandru…' he breathed harshly.

'Have you lost anything? Or should I say anyone?'

'How do you *know* that?' Alissandru demanded rawly.

'Because I've found what you lost by the side of the road, complete with a yappy little dog.'

'By the side of the road?' Alissandru exclaimed, leaping upright in consternation.

'The getaway car broke down,' Grazia said succinctly. 'I drove past them on the way home, had to practically force Isla into my car. What have you been doing, Alissandru?'

'I screwed up,' Alissandru bit out in a roughened undertone.

'Well, they're at my house and I'm off to my parents' for the night. Keys in the usual place. Admit it… I'm the best friend you've ever had.'

'You're the best friend I've ever had,' Alissandru recited breathlessly as he practically ran down the stairs, slammed through the door, flung himself into his car.

'Now stop right there and *think*,' Grazia urged as he fired the engine. 'You don't go in cold and without knowing what you're going to say.'

'I know. I know exactly,' Alissandru told her boldly, and he did know, just the same way as his twin had once told him he knew, only it had taken an awful lot longer for the truth to hit Alissandru.

But the truth had hit him at remarkable speed when he'd walked through that empty house and the prospect of spending even one night without Isla had hung over him like a thunderclap of doom.

Emotionally speaking, Isla was all over the place. She had had the strength to walk away and then Tania's car had broken down halfway between the estate and San Matteo. That was when the floods of tears had engulfed her. That was when everything going wrong had just combined into one giant heavy rock grinding her down, squeezing the life out of her. But above all had been the screaming sense of having left part of herself behind, as well.

She *loved* Alissandru Rossetti. She hated him for feeling sorry for her and neglecting to tell her about the will, but he was still the father of her baby and the man she loved. When Grazia had stopped and initially offered her a lift into town, Isla had had no choice but to accept the offer, and when she had asked if Grazia knew anywhere she could get a room for the night with a dog, Grazia had informed her that there was only one place. And she hadn't explained until she'd pulled up outside a beautiful, newish-looking, modern detached house outside town that the only place that would take a dog for the night was *her* house.

Practically pushing Isla through the front door, Grazia had then shown her up to an en-suite bedroom, urging her to get into something comfortable while telling her that the kitchen was full of food and to make herself at home.

Puggle had required no such encouragement. He had curled up in a basket in the kitchen with Grazia's elegant little grey whippet, Primo, and gone straight to sleep, the trauma of being pushed into his transport carrier gratefully left behind him.

Isla had showered and put on her pyjamas. She wasn't hungry and she wasn't sleepy either and the prospect of watching Italian television when she couldn't speak the language had little appeal. When she heard the front door opening, she assumed it was Grazia returning from wherever she had rushed off to, and she stood up. The sight of Alissandru walking through the door was a total shock and her eyes flew wide.

'How did you know I was here?' she gasped.

'Grazia. She knew I'd want to know. I owe her a massive thank you,' Alissandru bit out harshly. 'How could you just run off like that? What on earth possessed you?'

'What else could I do in the circumstances?' Isla hurled back. 'How did you think I'd feel when I found out about the second will? Where was it anyway?'

'Paulu's assistant found it in the contents of his desk... Look, sit down. You shouldn't be getting all riled up,' Alissandru framed jerkily, shaken to look at her and appreciate that she was carrying his child again, even more shaken by how that made him feel. It made him feel better; it made him feel that he had a future again.

'Why shouldn't I be getting all riled up?' Isla asked combatively. 'You withheld vital information from me. Information that I had a right to know.'

Alissandru yanked loose his bow tie and undid his collar while expelling his breath slowly. He didn't look as knife-sharp elegant and self-contained as he usually did. His black hair was untidy and lines of strain bracketed his mouth. He stared at her with glittering golden eyes. 'Where were you going when the car broke down?'

'I was hoping to find a hotel that would take Puggle but Grazia said there wasn't one that she knew of and brought me here. Then she just disappeared.'

'She's gone to her parents' for the night,' Alissandru explained and he stalked round the room, stopped to shrug and then looked at her again. 'How was I supposed to tell you about the second will? I knew it would wreck all your plans. I knew it would make you leave Sicily and that you wouldn't accept my financial help. I didn't *want* you to leave.'

'I'm leaving,' Isla told him, dry-mouthed. 'I have to deal with this situation and get on with my life. I may be pregnant but I'm not living off you unless I'm forced to.'

'*Expect* to be forced,' Alissandru muttered half under his breath while scooping up Puggle and ruffling his curly head with a wry apology for not having a treat for him. 'You see, if you're Puggle, life is simple. He trusts and likes the people who feed him.'

'I don't need you to feed me, Alissandru,' Isla said drily, while watching in surprise as he stroked her dog. 'When did you start liking him?'

He set the dog down. 'I wouldn't go as far as saying I like him yet, but he's yours and that makes a difference. He accepts me, I accept him.' He glanced at her through the tangle of his long black lashes, golden eyes bright as sunlight. 'I *want* this baby... I really, really *want* this baby. By the time I warmed up to the idea of the first baby, it was gone.'

'I didn't know you'd warmed up,' Isla whispered shakily, thoroughly disconcerted by what he had declared.

'You didn't give me the chance to tell you,' he reminded her. 'You just shut me out after the...miscarriage. I didn't think you'd believe me if I told you how I felt or that I was grieving, too. It was a loss to me, as well. I'd started looking forward to becoming a father, seeing the whole situation in a very positive light. But what restricted me back then doesn't restrict me now.'

Her brow furrowed as she tried to accept that he had felt much more than she had given him credit for when she'd miscarried. But she could not doubt the sincerity in his eyes or the husky emotion lacing his words. 'What restricted you?'

'I still had you all tangled up with Tania inside my head back then. I didn't trust you, didn't really know you. That's all changed,' he pointed out.

'Yes. But after the miscarriage, you said that it wasn't meant to be, and that really upset me,' she admitted unevenly. 'I assumed you meant that people like you and me, from such different backgrounds, don't have children together.'

His ebony brows pleated. 'Of course, I didn't mean that. I'm not a snob. I don't rate people by how much money they have.'

'You did me,' she reminded him helplessly.

'Tania cast a long shadow,' he said ruefully in his own defence. 'And I received a bad first impression of you. I didn't want to make the same mistake Paulu had and get involved with the wrong woman. That's why I left the croft so fast that morning. I wanted to stay longer. I wanted to spend time with you and that shocked me. I thought I'd soon get over it but after you, I didn't want other women. You spoiled me for them. I've only been with you since that first night.'

Genuine joy unfurled inside Isla at that unexpected assurance. She had wondered, of course she'd wondered whether he had been with anyone else before she came to Sicily. The discovery that he had only been with her made her feel much more secure.

That he wanted their baby as well and was willing to openly acknowledge the fact warmed her down deep inside.

'When I stood in that empty house tonight, I was devastated that you were gone and I knew then that I loved you and that nothing but marriage would satisfy me this time around.'

It was quite a speech and it shook Isla where she stood. She blinked and swallowed hard and when she looked again he was still studying her as if she was the only woman in the world for him. 'You love me? You want to marry me?'

'You once said you wouldn't marry me if I was the last man alive. I hope I've risen a little higher in your estimation since then,' he confided with entirely surprising humility as, to her shock, he got down on one knee.

'Marry me, Isla,' he urged. 'I do love you, more than I ever thought I could love any woman. Unfortunately you came into my life when I wasn't expecting you but having you in my life means everything to me and I don't want to lose you.'

Absolutely gobsmacked, Isla stared down at him without words, in such shock that she was reeling. 'You really love me?'

'I started falling for you the first night but I didn't realise why I couldn't forget you. So, will you marry me? I'm starting to feel like a bit of an idiot down here!' he told her drily.

'Of course, I'm going to marry you,' Isla informed him with newly learned confidence as she hauled him up to her with greedy hands. 'You love me, you want me, you want our baby…that's the biggest surprise of all!'

'A piece of you, a piece of me, maybe even a dash of my brother or even Tania,' Alissandru pointed out with only the faintest flinch at that final possibility. 'How could I not want my child? It took me a long time to get here, Isla, but now you've got me, you're not going to get rid of me again.'

Isla stood in the strong circle of his arms, trying to compute how life could travel from being totally horrendous to totally wonderful in the space of minutes, and not doing very well. 'I don't want rid of you,' she mumbled shakily, and then the tears were coming, cascading from her eyes as though she had taps behind them.

And Alissandru grabbed her up in a panic and sank down on the sofa holding her. 'What's wrong?'

'I'm j-just s-so h-happy!' Isla stammered apologetically through her tears.

'But you're crying,' Alissandru said gently as though she might not have noticed.

Isla gave an inelegant sniff. 'I think it's my hormones. I think it's being pregnant.'

Alissandru was bewildered. 'So…you're happy? You're *definitely* going to marry me?'

'Obviously.' She gulped. 'You're not usually this stupid.'

'I've never been in love before. Never been with a woman who would dare to call me stupid, either,' Alissandru admitted with a spontaneous laugh.

'Well, of course, you're going to be stupid sometimes,' Isla told him briskly, having finally mastered the tears dripping down her face. 'But, you know, you're not the only one who fell in love this spring. I love you too, but this time I thought we were only having an affair because you kept on hinting that we weren't going to last for ever.'

'That was the last dying strands of the single guy trying to stay free,' Alissandru told her with wry amusement in his gaze. 'Paulu told me once I didn't know what love was and he was right. I would forgive you just about anything…but now don't take that as an invitation,' he added with his usual caution.

'Are you really happy about the baby? How do you think it happened?'

'I haven't got a clue and don't care. I'm just delighted that it has,' Alissandru confided with warmth glowing in his level dark golden eyes.

'I'm scared that something will go wrong again,' Isla confided in a rush.

'We both are, but at least we're together now and *together* we can handle anything,' Alissandru said with confidence. 'I've got you and a whole future with you waiting for me…and I've never been happier in my whole life than I feel at this moment.'

That was quite a declaration from the once cynical love of her life and Isla rested her head back against his shoulder, struggling to accept that such wondrous happiness could finally be hers. 'I love you,' she whispered, stroking a fingertip along his shapely upper lip. 'And we're going to be incredibly good together.'

Alissandru smiled down at her with such tenderness in his beautiful eyes that her heart squeezed tight as the hold she had on him. This man with all his emotion would love strong and true, she sensed, thinking of his care for his own family. They had travelled a rocky road to their happy ending but they had both learned a lot on the journey. Her whole life was now opening up into a new dimension and the knowledge that she was no longer alone was a great source of joy to her. Alissandru and a baby too, she thought blissfully…

Almost four years later, Isla presided over a Christmas spent in London in their town house, which was filled to capacity with dogs and children. Indeed,

Alissandru was talking about looking for a larger house as a London base.

'I just don't know how you've managed to acquire four of them so fast,' Grazia pronounced, eying the four children surrounding Constantia with astonishment. 'Thank heaven, I'm only having one,' she added, patting the swell of her stomach beneath her highly trendy mint-green dress.

'Two sets of twins adds to the count,' Isla pointed out with amusement sparkling in her eyes, for Grazia, who had become a dear friend, had only married the year before and motherhood was entirely new to her. Entering an environment cluttered with the paraphernalia of *four* young children was more than a little daunting for her.

Gerlanda and Cettina had been born first—identical twins, dark haired and blue-eyed, two very lively little girls now three years old. Luciu and Grazzianu were non-identical boys and still babies, one noisy and demanding like his father but with red hair, the other quieter and more contented and dark. They had truly planned their third pregnancy although they hadn't planned on a second set of twins.

Isla's favourite photograph of their wedding sat near the fire, ring-fenced by a guard to protect the children. It showed her gorgeous traditional wedding dress, which had been nowhere near as trendy as poor Grazia had wanted to make it but had been everything that Isla had dreamt of, which was exactly as it *should* be, Grazia had said of a bride's gown. Her uncle had given her away at their beautiful Sicilian summer wedding and it had been a wonderful family day, her relatives as welcome as the Rossetti clan could make them.

It was hard for Isla to credit that she had been married to Alissandru for almost four years. While she was pregnant with the girls she had done the London course she had wanted to do to complete her education to her own satisfaction. That achieved, she had discovered that she was happy to be a stay-at-home mother with a bunch of kids and dogs because she liked to be available when Alissandru was at home. He didn't travel as much as he once had and he was always home at weekends and holidays, she thought fondly, watching Alissandru lift his youngest son in his arms and talk with apparent confidence about his feeding schedule. As if *he* had anything to do with it, Isla ruminated with amusement. They had a nanny to help and Alissandru got more involved with the fun side of parenting like bathtime and bedtime and buying toys. My goodness, could that man buy toys!

That had possibly been the biggest surprise of

their marriage, Isla conceded with a tender smile. Alissandru adored kids, adored her being pregnant and wanted more. And she had told him no, four was *enough* and he would just have to content himself with four.

They spent most of their time now in Sicily and Isla could speak the language, although she made a fair number of mistakes, which she could depend on Alissandru to always correct. Sometimes, she thought ruefully, he was the most annoying man and yet if anything, after four years, he owned even more of her heart than he had at the outset of their marriage. He treated her as if she were as fragile as glass and tried to protect her from anything that he deemed prejudicial to her state of mind.

He strode over to her, clutching Grazzianu to his chest like a well-wrapped parcel. 'He's ready for his nap.'

As he bent his dark head down to her she saw the devilment in his gaze and knew that the only person ready for a nap was Alissandru and it *wasn't* a nap he meant. She collected Luciu from his adoring grandmother and they took the babies upstairs to the nursery to settle them into their cots.

'I… I just wanted to give you this,' Alissandru confessed, surprising her as he loved to do, wrapping a diamond necklace round her throat like a choker and fixing the clasp before she could object. 'You thought I meant sex,' he said piously, as if such an idea would never have occurred to him.

'It's not even Christmas Day yet!' Isla exclaimed, ignoring that crack.

'I love buying you stuff. I love that you can't say no now, *mia bella*,' Alissandru confided, tugging her close to his lean, powerful frame.

'I have more diamonds than I know what to do with,' she muttered repressively, thinking of the king's ransom in jewellery he had given her and the shelves and shelves of glorious handmade silk and lace lingerie, which she was willing to admit that she enjoyed wearing. 'But thank you very, very much,' she whispered, because she knew it was his way of showing how much he loved her and that she couldn't change him and wouldn't have changed him even if she could have done.

'But you're the most precious diamond of all,' Alissandru intoned huskily. 'I just adore you.'

And Isla smiled with the tremendous warmth that had attracted him from the very first time he saw that smile, he acknowledged thankfully. She was the centre of his world and all the sunshine in it, and the idea that he might have walked on by and missed out on what he had found with her still terrified him in retrospect.

'And you know you're loved…or you ought to,' Isla informed him, kissing that smoothly shaven jaw line, which was as far up as she could reach, thinking how different he felt unshaven as he had been at dawn and as hot and rampant as only Alissandru could be and making her equally so.

'I like to be told occasionally,' Alissandru countered, taking a stand.

'Why don't I *show* you instead?' Isla whispered, watching those stunning eyes of his light up with alacrity and smiling even more.

* * * * *

If you enjoyed
The Italian's Inherited Mistress
you're sure to enjoy these other stories
by Lynne Graham!

The Secret Valtinos Baby
Castiglione's Pregnant Princess
Da Rocha's Convenient Heir
The Billionaire's Blackmailed Mistress

Available now!

COMING NEXT MONTH FROM
H HARLEQUIN
Presents.

Available December 18, 2018

#3681 THE SECRET KEPT FROM THE ITALIAN
Secret Heirs of Billionaires
by Kate Hewitt

Rejected after one mind-blowing night, Maisie kept her pregnancy a secret. Now Antonio's determined to claim his daughter. But their connection reminds Maisie that she still has to protect her heart—because billionaires don't wed waitresses...do they?

#3682 CARRYING THE SHEIKH'S BABY
One Night With Consequences
by Heidi Rice

When shy Cat is hired by Sheikh Zane, she's thrilled—and completely dazzled by their overwhelming chemistry! But their passionate encounter has lasting consequences, and carrying Zane's heir means one thing—Cat must become his queen!

#3683 THE TYCOON'S SHOCK HEIR
by Bella Frances

Restoring his family's legacy is all that's important to Matteo. Yet when Ruby confesses she's pregnant, Matteo demands his child. But with heat still burning between them, can Matteo ignore his desire for Ruby, too?

#3684 THE SPANIARD'S UNTOUCHED BRIDE
Brides of Innocence
by Maisey Yates

Camilla refuses to abandon her beloved horses when Matias acquires her family's *rancho*. Instead, she disguises herself as his stable boy! Yet when Camilla's charade is discovered, Matias offers her an even more shocking role—as his wife!

HPCNM1218RA

#3685 MY BOUGHT VIRGIN WIFE

Conveniently Wed!

by Caitlin Crews

I've never wanted anything like I want Imogen. I married her to secure my empire—but my wife has ignited a hunger in me. I will strip away her obedience, and replace it with a passion to match my own...

#3686 AWAKENING HIS INNOCENT CINDERELLA

by Natalie Anderson

Gracie is mortified when Rafaele finds her accidentally trespassing on his estate! She can't refuse Rafe's teasing demand that she attend an exclusive party with him. Can she resist the power of his raw sensuality?

#3687 CLAIMED FOR THE BILLIONAIRE'S CONVENIENCE

by Melanie Milburne

When headlines mistakenly announce Holly's engagement to Zack, she's stunned. Yet Zack seems determined to turn this scandal, and their red-hot attraction, to their mutual advantage...

#3688 ONE NIGHT WITH THE FORBIDDEN PRINCESS

Monteverro Marriages

by Amanda Cinelli

Facing an arranged marriage, runaway Princess Olivia pleads with billionaire bodyguard Roman to allow her just one week of freedom. But secluded on his private island, their forbidden attraction is explosively undeniable!

Jealousy fired through Antonio, although he couldn't even say why. So Maisie had moved on, found a boyfriend or husband and had a baby pretty darn quick. That was fine. Of course it was. Except...

They'd spent the night together a year ago, and although Antonio wasn't an expert on babies by any means, the child nestled in the man's arms looked to be at least a few months old. Which meant...

Either Maisie had been pregnant when she'd slept with him, or had fallen pregnant immediately after. Or, he realized with a sickening rush, had become pregnant by him.

Don't miss
The Secret Kept from the Italian,
available January 2019 wherever
Harlequin Presents® books and ebooks are sold.

www.Harlequin.com

*Rejected after one mind-blowing night, Maisie kept her
pregnancy a secret. Now Antonio's determined to claim
his daughter. But their connection reminds Maisie that
she still has to protect her heart—because billionaires
don't wed waitresses...do they?*

*Read on for a sneak preview of
Kate Hewitt's next story,*
The Secret Kept from the Italian

"Maisie."

Antonio looked up at the sound of her name on another
man's lips. The man was standing by the entrance to the
hotel, a smile on his face as he held out his arms. Slowly
Antonio turned and saw Maisie walking toward the man,
a tremulous smile curving her lush lips, a baby nestled in
her arms.

A baby.

Antonio stared as the man took the baby from her,
cuddling the little bundle as he cooed down at it.

"Hey, sweetie."